HOUSE OF OZ UNDONE

HOUSE

of

OZ

a cautionary tale

UNDONE

ELEANOR L. TOMCZYK

HOUSE OF OZ UNDONE
First Edition Eleanor L. Tomczyk

Published by
Howthehelldidienduphere? Publications LLC

Papernack ISBN: 978-1-960299-43-7
Hardcover ISBN: 978-1-960299-44-4
Printed in the United States of America

"There are six things the Lord hates, seven that are detestable to him: haughty eyes, a lying tongue, hands that shed innocent blood, a heart that devises wicked schemes, feet that are quick to rush into evil, a false witness who pours out lies, and a person who stirs up conflict in the community."

—Proverbs 6:16-19 (NIV Bible)

For the Truth Seekers
and
My Grandchildren's Generation

CONTENTS

Chapter I

The Golf Cart Tango

They say life is what happens to you when you're on your way to somewhere else. As a Black woman having spent sixty-five years on this planet, I can pretty much attest to that. A few of my life happenings have been pleasant, but most of the time, they have been rude awakenings—the kind that grab you by the throat, punch you in the gut, and turn you inside out—leaving you shell-shocked and barely able to breathe.

Someone murdered my best friend.

We had been friends since our kindergarten days when we both lived in Hole in the Wall, Kansas, as we dismissively called our home town. Sixty years we'd loved and trusted each other. Jonathan "Glinda" Dubois was like no other human being I'd ever met—the most loving, the most joyful, the most guileless, the most loyal, and the most beautiful individual I'd been blessed to call my friend. As kids, Jonathan had always known he wanted to be a drag queen, and I had always wanted to be a jazz singer.

"We were born to be entertainers, Chica," Jonathan would say. "Don't you never no mind that there's no drag club or jazz scene within a thousand miles from this Kansas hellhole we were born in because

"

someday I'll be headlining as the exquisite *Porcelain Doll, Glinda Dubois,* and you'll be giving the legacy of the *Sassy and Divine One, Miss Sarah Vaughan,* a run for her money, honey."

She would always see the look of skepticism on my face, and she'd never fail to say to me: *"Don't give up, Miss Fine Thang. Stay loving, stay caring, stay humble, and the good things of life will lift you into the place where you belong."*

"Right back at you, girlfriend," I'd reply, never quite believing my wish would ever come true.

I was on my way to someplace else when I got the call from a lawyer that Jonathan was dead. And unbeknownst to me, he had left me his home in a fifty-five-plus retirement community in the heart of Texas, as well as his precious one-year-old Bichon Frisé puppy, Toe-Toe, along with a warning note about both of his "blessings" to me.

Dear Chica: If you're reading this note, then I am definitely dead! I recently had some issues with being harassed and bullied, and to such a serious extent that I decided to make this will in case the threats made against my life came to fruition. I'm not afraid of dying, Chica—I'm just afraid of dying before Toe-Toe does, and her being without a home. I know we haven't seen each other in years, and we've lost touch with each other, but you're my only family, and I know you still love me, as I do you.

First, I leave you my house. You've always been a nomad so it might feel strange for you to settle down in one place. You're an old woman now, and you can't keep bus-and-trucking it to every low-rent club in the nation to sing and then return to your rented one-bedroom lackluster apartment in Kansas. (How's that for getting a scolding from the beyond?) Feel free to sell the house and buy another someplace else, but if you do decide to settle down here, there are a few things you need to know about your new home and your new baby.

My house is in a master-planned community that's on steroids! It's based on **The Wonderful Wizard of Oz***—replete with a Glinda castle in the* *south. I had planned to move to that section soon, but buying my current home got my foot in the door of this L. Frank Baum wet dream. I currently live in Munchkinville country in the magical Land of Oz. You're going to think it's over-the-top when you see the place—everything from the Wicked Witch of the West quadrant to the Emerald City mansions. However, you know me, I'm a sucker for all things Glinda. Oz Heritage Settlement used to be a blast when I first moved here, although it has turned a little weird lately. I completely understand, if after trying it out, you decide to sell— but do give it a chance, my love.*

What is completely non-negotiable is whether to keep Toe-Toe or not. I know you don't do dogs, but we promised to go to the ends of the Earth for each other, and you can consider the act of adopting Toe-Toe your Earth's end for me. I love that puppy more than my life, Dottie. Please keep my baby safe and healthy. May you both live long and bring each other great joy. May you become family. See you on the other side, girlfriend!

"*Oy vez iz mir!* Jonathan, what have you gotten me into?" I thought, as I waited in a veterinarian's office to find out why Toe-Toe wasn't eating, wasn't pooping, and had tried to die by suicide by trying to gnaw off her right leg when I left her for an hour to go to the dentist.

"If you can hear me, sweetheart," I muttered into the air, "your dog incessantly cries and refuses to sleep in her bed, but insists on sleeping on top of my head, and when she does, she pees all over it. She won't pee outside, but she can cut loose like a broken dam on my head. You've known all your life that I don't do dogs. God, I'm about to lose my mind!"

The old man sitting next to me moved away, probably thinking I was crazy. As he now sat across the room, I noticed for the first time the campaign poster above his head: "GMOMA: VOTE FOR THE PURPLE WICKED WITCH OF THE WEST, IF YOU WANT TO SAVE OZ!"

As I was trying to figure out what GMOMA stood for, the vet's office door opened and I was summoned.

"Hello, Miss Gale, I'm Dr. Hauptmann—pleased to meet you," said the most sanguine human being I'd ever met. "Welcome to Oz. Are you settling in all right?"

"Pleasure's all mine, Doc, especially if you can heal this poor excuse of a dog," I replied, as he enthusiastically pumped my hand up and down at rapid speed.

"Hey, I saw a campaign sign in your office that I don't understand," I said. "Somebody's running for office around here?"

"Not just somebody," whispered the Dog Whisperer. The air seemed to escape out of all the orifices on his head as he deflated in front of me and became very taciturn.

"It's the Wicked Witch of the West—known around these parts as The Purple One," said the vet. "She's running for the presidency of Oz —it would be a second term. But this time around, she's campaigning to be president for life. *God help us all!*"

"Really? What do the initials GMOMA mean?"

"Go Make Oz Magnificent Again!"

"Seriously?" I asked. "I was under the impression you guys thought this place was already pretty sweet. Everyone I meet seems absolutely orgasmic to be living in Oz."

"Not all of us," said the vet in a *sotto voce* manner. "Not anymore."

Then, as if someone had slapped him across the face, the animal doctor said, "Enough about politics. Let's talk about Toe-Toe, shall we?"

"Oh yeah, the dog from Hell," I replied, with a sigh of exasperation.

"*Toe-Toe* . . . Looks like my receptionist spelled her name incorrectly."

"No, Doc. Her diva mother registered the spelling of her name that way because this damn dog *won't* go outside to do her business on the grass or concrete. She also *won't* pee or poop outside if it's below 60 degrees or above 80 degrees. And she has the nerve to do all these *won'ts* on her tiptoes as if she deigned to walk completely on the feet God gave her, they would instantly combust. Not to mention, Toe-Toe turns her nose up at her food and throws up every other day. God forbid someone sets off firecrackers—which they seem to do every evening here—Miss T.T. will scamper up the side of my body like a cat chasing a squirrel up a tree and perch herself on top of my Vivica Fox wig as if my head were her private dog loft. She's very clingy. I can't even go to the bathroom without her attached to my leg! Oh, and if I give her a disappointed look when she's done something that gets on my nerves, she engages in destructive behavior like trying to chew off her leg."

"Well, I've had a long talk with Miss Toe-Toe, and she confided in me that she's depressed," said the vet. "She finds her new living arrangements totally unacceptable and her new mommy a tad bit lacking in the canine knowledge department—her words, not mine. She also says you can hardly get out of your own way and that her real mommy must have lost her freakin' mind making you her guardian. Pardon my language.

"What's that, Toe-Toe?" continued the vet. "You could use a pedicure and a spa day? Maybe have your toes painted rainbow colors as a treat?"

Toe-Toe effusively barked several times as if she were officially signing off on each of the vet's suggestions.

"Bullshit! This dog can't talk. You're making this shit up!" I replied as I laughed at the absurdity of this vet translating for a puffball.

"Well, they don't call me the Dog Whisperer for nothing," he said with a twinkle in his eye as he looked down and winked at Toe-Toe. "Seriously, I suggest we put Toe-Toe on puppy Prozac for her low mood, change her food for her delicate tummy to the gourmet canned variety that can only be purchased from our firm, and that you two go on a little vacation together—just the two of you for emotional connection. Maybe a road trip? Something to build your relationship after the demise of Toe-Toe's mommy. See you next week for a follow-up."

"That will be $650.00 for today's visit," said the chirpy receptionist. As I shot laser beams of scorn at her, she sheepishly said: "Well, look on the bright side, today's your lucky day. Our gourmet dog food, which normally costs $50 for a 16-ounce can, is on sale for $48.99."

As I stormed out of the Vet's office to my golf cart—the only mode of transportation allowed in this planned community, which is usually driven by a bunch of senior citizens who start drinking Mimosas by 10 in the morning—Princess Toe-Toe pranced behind me on her tippy-toes looking like she'd rather be anywhere but here, as I lost my shit.

"*Depressed?* I'm the one who's depressed! Please! *Prozac?* You better share some of those drugs with me, cause I'm losing my mind in this Oz place. *Road trip for a dog?* Child, you must think I'm a White mother with money to burn. *You're a dog, for Christ's sake!* You should be guarding my shit, not draining my bank account. Get your vanilla, snowball, tiptoeing ass into this golf cart before I have a good mind to leave your precious butt with that froufrou vet and risk being haunted by your mommy for the rest of my life.

"Jesus! I hate this fake, nothing-better-to-do-with-your-money-than-waste-it community. I've only been here a short while but I'm already so tired of boozy bingo, endless rounds of pickleball and bridge games, pitchers of margaritas before noon, and country line dancing to Toby Keith's 'As Good As I Once Was,' until I drop from exhaustion at the House of the Rich Boq Bar and Grill, that I could scream!

"Toe-Toe, what did your mommy see in this place? Not one of Jonathan's neighbors has dropped by to say hello. Not one religious leader has offered me condolences over Jonathan's death even though there's a church on every corner. And not one police officer has followed up on my inquiries about how Jonathan died. *I've got real problems here,* Pooch, and a doctor—albeit a veterinarian—never even asked about *my* health and well-being, but had the nerve to engage in psychic powers with *you* and charge me a king's ransom for it."

At that moment of strapping Toe-Toe into the passenger seat of the golf cart, a woman passed me in the parking lot, lost in her own world, wearing a T-shirt that could have been the mission statement of Oz

Heritage Settlement: *If you DON'T need anything today, then I am here for YOU!*"

Jesus, shoot me now.

The traffic was unusually congested going back to Jonathan's house. Our ordinary-looking golf cart was dwarfed by the souped-up, customized carts that were miniature replicas of everything from Rolls Royces to Hummers.

I couldn't believe this Oz place was for real. Jonathan never told me much about his new home because he probably thought I'd tease him until the cows came home. Only White people could think of wasting money on something as ludicrous as living in a planned, gated community that was the size of Brooklyn with fifty golf courses, three-hundred pickleball courts, sixty swimming pools, one thousand social clubs, scores of beauty parlors and spas, a hundred movie theaters, a bar on every other block, and a fuckin' yellow brick road that ran throughout Oz from one end of the settlement to the imperial gates of Emerald City. This place was definitely 98.9 percent White, and I could only guess that the other 1.1 percent must have been a math error because I was the only African American I'd seen in Munchkinville. There may have been one or two in other quadrants of Oz, but I hadn't heard of them. It was quite apparent by the hostile stares from the people in town that I was not welcome there.

My morose contemplation was suddenly interrupted when Toe-Toe cut loose an ear-splitting string of hysterical barks in my direction. Then she froze in terror at the sight of a monster golf cart barreling down on us. Both our mouths widened in horror as the top of the front wheels of the biggest souped-up golf cart rose up in the air to crush us. It was the Hummer golf cart to beat all souped-up carts. As I wrapped Toe-Toe in my arms and cushioned her between my massive triple Ds, the last thing I saw as the Hummer cart rolled up over our cart was its bumper sticker. It read: "OZ! JUST ANOTHER DAY IN PARADISE!"

CHAPTER II

Dottie Meets the Council from the Group of Concerned Citizens

"Miss Gale? Miss Gale?" said a man as he shook my right shoulder. "Open your eyes . . . that a girl. Come on now. Focus. Let me see those beautiful brown eyes."

I woke up in a shock and popped straight up like a jack-in-the-box before promptly collapsing back down on a pillow. My head seemed to be splitting wide open from the pain, and I could barely move it on my neck. As my vision came more into focus, I seemed to be in a hospital room with three pint-sized men and an even shorter woman whispering amongst themselves.

I tried to obey the doctor's instructions as he shone a penlight in my eyes but every inch of my body was in excruciating pain, including my eyelids.

"Miss Gale, I'm Dr. Ragosin, head of the neurological department of the Ma'on Center," said the unusually short man in the white coat. "You were brought here after being involved in a road rage accident. Do you remember anything about the incident? Do you know where you are? Do you know what date it is?"

"No, no, and no! Who is Miss Gale?" I asked, as I tried to sit up again and cradled my aching head in my hands.

"That's your name, dear," said the roly-poly woman. "Do you remember your address?"

I looked up at her and began to panic as I tried to reach for something in my brain that I suspected should have been floating around in there, but it eluded my grasp. I hopelessly shook my head in the negative.

"According to the town registrar's office, your name is Dorothy "Dottie" Hope Gale—may I call you Dottie? And you took over the house of Jonathan "Glinda" Dubois—such a lovely man," said the roly-poly woman. "We always had tea together whenever I came to town."

"I—I know who Jonathan is—he's my friend. I remember coming down here for the reading of Jonathan's will, but everything else is foggy. How did I get here—in a hospital?"

"You were involved in a very bad accident on the Right Way Highway this morning, which killed Mrs. Ernestine Early," said the short man in a blue uniform.

"What? No, no, no, no, no . . . I may not know my name, but I think I'd know if I killed someone."

"According to the eyewitnesses, Ernestine Early technically killed herself when she tried to kill you," said the police officer.

"*Say what?*"

"She's president of the Neighborhood Watch, and she makes it her personal vendetta to rid Munchkinville of residents she doesn't like or she thinks don't fit in," said the police officer. "Most everybody and everything in Munchkinville is under her control–except yours truly. In fact, she could have an Academy Award for being the biggest, nosey busybody. She's cruel, she's mean, and she's a bitch! Around these parts, we call her the Wicked Witch of the East. I suspect the residents will be so happy she's gone that they will throw you a ticker-tape parade. What's more, according to eyewitnesses, Early tried to sideswipe you but after hitting your golf cart, she overcorrected her Hummer cart, and it flipped and slid down the embankment she was trying to push you over. Her cart ultimately landed on top of her and squished her like a roach. I know it's not professional to say so but it seems like poetic justice to me."

"Excuse me, Miss Gale. Just a few questions, please. I'm a reporter from the *Emerald City Chronicle*," said the third man in the room. "Do you have a clue why you were on Ernestine Early's hit list?"

"I can't even remember my name, I don't ever remember even meeting this wretched woman, and I certainly can't imagine why she'd hate me," I replied with no small amount of irritation. "Although I do remember my friend Jonathan, but not much else."

"Hmm, then why were you brought in wearing Ernestine Early's shoes?" queried the reporter. "Everyone in town knows what Witch Early's shoes look like—they were designed specifically for her. One of a kind. I once did a story just on her special shoes. Did you steal them?"

"What? Listen, I may not be able to tell you my name and address, but I haven't lost my soul. I could never kill anyone and I am not a thief!"

I looked down at my feet for the first time since waking up and saw a pair of enclosed, bejeweled, silver clogs adorning them. They were bedazzled with sequins and rhinestones, so much so, that one could have seen them from the moon. I tried to push them off my feet by rubbing them against each other, but they wouldn't budge.

Seeing how agitated the reporter's questions had made me, Dr. Ragosin whispered to them all to leave except for the woman who turned out to be a patient ombudswoman from the North. The doctor then diagnosed me with transient global amnesia—short-term memory loss due to trauma. He said I shouldn't be alarmed, that my memory should return shortly—bit by bit. The munchkin doctor then said he wasn't so much worried about my memory as what he perceived to be an aura of despair that hung over my persona, which was not his area of expertise. He suggested that I go see a therapist once my memory returned. The doctor then left me in the spiritual care of the grand-motherly patient advocate.

After we both sat for a long time in silence as she stared at me in utter bemusement, the ombudswoman finally spoke: "Dear, I think you ought to go to the City of Emeralds and visit the Wizard of Oz. His given name is The Right Reverend Emerald, the Divine, but through the years, he's simply become known as The Wizard. He prides himself on guarding the truth and restoring minds, hearts, and souls. I've never been to see him myself, but others swear by him. You seem to need more than your memory returned. You seem to be yearning to get back to something or someone.

"Plus, it's not safe for you here. Somehow, you mysteriously ended up with the Wicked Witch of the East's shoes on your feet, which were her prized possessions. She never wore any other pair. In all the years I've known her, they never needed replacing. I do believe that they have a bit of magic about them, but what it is, I've never known. I do know that the Wicked Witch of the West has always coveted them, which means it won't be long before she comes looking for Ernestine's shoes once word reaches the West Witch that the East Witch is dead. I'll send one of my trusted nurses to accompany you to the City of Emeralds because I don't think you'd be capable of finding it on your own in your condition. It is an arduous journey, full of all sorts of evil, and a lot of unknowns. The road that leads to the City of Emeralds is paved with yellow bricks, so it won't be too hard to find."

"Will you please come with me?" I asked.

"No, this journey is your destiny, not mine. But who knows, maybe you'll meet some companions along the way seeking their own answers from the Wizard. Goodbye. May the God Ma'on give you safe travels, my dear!"

With that blessing, the ombudswoman leaned down and kissed me on the forehead. I felt a tingly sensation on my face—as if I were indelibly marked with the grace of a good witch from the North.

Chapter III

Dottie and a Woman Without a Brain
Get the Hell Out of Dodge

I don't know how long I'd been sleeping, but when I woke up this time, it was not from the shaking of my shoulder by a munchkin doctor, but from the frantic licking of my face by a nappy-headed white dog who seemed to be willing me awake with every lick.

"Toe-Toe," I screamed, "you're alive!"

"You remember you have a dog and you remember her name. Excellent!" said the nurse sitting next to my bed. "My aunt will be so pleased."

"Your aunt?" I said while trying to figure out who this person was.

"My Aunt Miranda," replied the nurse. "She was the ombudswoman you met yesterday, and I am the person she tasked with accompanying you to the Emerald City.

"Hi, my name is Maria Espantapájaro. My side gig is assisting my aunt's clients with whatever they need on their journeys to be restored. I'm a registered nurse and a great driver if you're feeling a bit squeamish about getting back into a golf cart again."

"Pleased to meet you, Maria," I said. "Where did you find my dog?"

"I found her wandering around the hospital parking lot. She looked really dazed and confused. Fortunately, I noticed the diamond choker with her name tag on it that listed you as the dog's owner. I recognized your name as it was the same one my aunt had sent me to escort to Emerald City."

"Come closer you little weird vanilla bean of a dog," I said, as I crushed Toe-Toe to my chest. "You look like you've been through hell. I don't remember you being the color of dust-bowl gray and your fur being a stand-in for sticky bristle grass. Good God, puppy, you better hope your mommy doesn't have the ability to haunt us or she's going to come back and kick both our asses.

"Did anyone check her over? Is she OK?"

"Yes, and yes," said Nurse Maria. "I had her checked out by the vet's office adjacent to the hospital. Nothing is broken—she's just a little bit shaken up is what they said. I know she looks less than ideal, but we've no time to waste to get her groomed. We've got to get going—Emerald City is quite a distance from here, and people will be searching for you."

"I feel so bad that I'm pulling you from your life. Do you have a family?"

"*Had* a husband. He thought he was God and I thought he wasn't. He blamed his reason for dumping me on my lack of a brain, and said— and I quote—'You have shit for brains.' It was the problem he found with most women. But that was a long time ago. Although, every once in a while, I'm plagued with the nagging notion that he may have been right. It does seem that my ability to think things through to their proper conclusion is only getting worse as I get older. At least it feels that way since my husband summarily cursed me. His accusation broke me, for sure. I guess I've done what a therapist might label as letting my abuser define me and accepting that definition as truth, which is why I'll gladly escort you to see the Wizard. Who knows, maybe The Wizard can give me a new brain, and prove my ex-husband wrong. I've tried every-thing else. We'll leave before the crack of dawn."

"I'm not sure Toe-Toe and I can get our asses in gear enough to take a trip anywhere except maybe to the toilet, and that's debatable," I said. "Look at us, we're a mangled mess! All we want to do is stay in this bed and cling to each other."

"Well, I wouldn't advise that. The sooner we get going, the sooner we'll get to Emerald City and get the help we both need. I'm a licensed physical therapist. I'll get you and Toe-Toe in tip-top shape before you can say: 'We're off to see the Wizard!'" said Maria as she laughed at the perfect timing of her corny joke.

We talked most of the day, as Maria massaged my banged-up body and put me through a strict regimen of stretching exercises to prepare me for the arduous journey ahead. While Maria twisted and stretched me, and I screamed and moaned, she recounted the story of how her great-grandfather—one of the co-founders of Oz Heritage Settlement— had dreamed of a community of people who had two things in common: they were senior citizens and they loved and were completely dedicated to the God, Ma'on. Back in the day, they called themselves the Children of Ma'on, which the ancients considered one of the many names for God. Maria explained that Ma'on meant refuge—a place of shelter from danger or hardship.

Turns out the Oz planning theme started out as a joke. One of the founders had a fondness for L. Frank Baum's book, **The Wonderful Wizard of Oz**, and he became intrigued with the unique marketing idea for like-minded seniors looking for a safe place to land while serving the great Ma'on. All were welcome—no matter where you were in your spiritual journey. All were included—just so long as you were fifty-five years and older. And all were to be governed by the same mission state- ment: *"Love your neighbor as yourself."* I could now see why Jonathan had been drawn to this community. It was the type of belonging he had been looking for all of his life.

Unfortunately, according to Nurse Maria, things started to go south almost immediately. One of the co-founders sought to elevate himself as supreme leader. The other founder slept with that co-founder's wife. Then the retirees who had been lured to an inclusive community began to sort themselves into the *haves* and the *have-nots*—the *us* and the *them* which made Oz ripe for a community take-over by anyone who wanted to manipulate the imagined grievances of the *us* group.

Soon individuality was frowned upon and sameness in thought, race, creed, and ethnicity were rewarded with power and citizenship within Oz.

Fast forward: The most effective rebels against Maria's great-grandfather's vision were those in the 1970s who managed to sneak in their children and grandchildren—mainly because they missed them. They reared them in Oz before a draconian homeowner's association finally put the kibosh on anyone under the age of fifty-five dwelling within its borders for more than a two-week visit. By that time, there was a significant group of under fifty-fives who were grandfathered in—including his own great-grandchild. Eventually, quite a few of the younger generations found Oz to be rather lame. Those that did, kicked Oz to the curb and left for greener pastures. A thousand or so never left the fairy tale land and became part of the massive service industry that catered to the geriatric residents.

I fell into a deep nightmarish sleep after hearing Maria's mournful recounting of the demise of a community that had started with such great spiritual and human promise. I dreamt about my friend Jonathan being tormented by the Wicked Witch of the East as I imagined she drove him to his death. I couldn't prove anything yet, but she was involved somehow, and her road rage vendetta had to be connected to Jonathan's murder.

I woke up before dawn and declared to Maria and Toe-Toe, "For the sake of my friend and your mommy's memory and last wishes, Toe-Toe, if we plan to live another day, we'd better get the hell out of Dodge!"

CHAPTER IV

Girls' Road Trip

"Where in Oz did you get this monstrosity?" I asked Maria as she pulled up to the back of the hospital in a souped-up golf cart that looked like a miniature jeep.

"There are still some perks for being the great-granddaughter of an Oz founder," she replied. "We'll need a sturdy vehicle if we have to go off-road. I've never traveled past the outskirts of Munchkinville on the Yellow Brick Road so I have no idea what condition the road is in between here and Emerald City.

"Plus, I needed plenty of room for our supplies. I picked up a couple blankets, boiled some eggs, stole some fruit and bottled water from the hospital kitchen, and bought some beef jerky and some dry dog food at the corner bodega. I 'borrowed' a satellite cell phone from the EMT unit. *Voilà*, I brought you a pair of readers from the pharmacy since I noticed you squinting while trying to read your medical chart this morning. Also, I brought you a couple of yoga outfits with a warm jacket from my closet. Looks like they'll fit."

"Look at you strategizing and using that noggin to think," I said as I laughed while trying to stuff myself into a yoga outfit that was two sizes too small and four inches too long. I was grateful for the long jacket after I rolled up the pants' hem and my muffin top popped out between the too-high crop top and the too-low, too-tight yoga pants. I then caught a glimpse of Toe-Toe's face as she stared at the bag of dry dog food—and rolled her eyes in disgust.

"Toe-Toe, part of our girls' road trip entails you turning over a new leaf—starting right now. It's coming back to me what an insufferable diva you are. I'm recalling our last conversation where I told you that I am a Black mama—not a permissive White mother. So, here's how we roll from now on: You either eat the food Maria and I provide for you or you go hungry—your choice. There will be no whining, no rolling of the eyes, and no refusal to poop and pee when the time comes. You understand me, bitch? And I say this with deep affection."

Maria tried to hide her laughter as Toe-Toe let out an explosive sigh of resignation—equivalent to a teenager's complaint of, *"Oh, man!"*—before getting comfortable on the blanket on the floor of the souped-up cart's back seat.

Connecting with the Yellow Brick Road was a simple task because it was the only major highway out of Munchkinville and it was paved with bright yellow bricks. As the sun began to rise in the sky, beautiful suburban mega mansions started to dot the landscape along with Purple Wicked Witch campaign signs:

"PURPLE WICKED WITCH, 2024, TAKE BACK OZ!"

"THE WICKED WITCH, 2024, MAKE VOTES COUNT AGAIN!"

"WICKED WITCH OF THE WEST, 2024, GO MAKE OZ MAGNIFICENT AGAIN!"

"I take it that Oz is having an election this year," I said to Maria, as we zipped along the yellow highway.

"Not just any old election—the presidential election to rule all of Oz. For the first time, a candidate is running for re-election on the platform of Ruler for Life. The Wicked Witch of the West wants to become an authoritarian ruler with total control of Oz so she can shape it into her vision of the perfect community."

"Would that be so bad?" I asked. "Didn't you tell me that Oz has fallen short of the glory of Ma'on, and it's no longer the community it started out to be?"

"It would be horrible because the Purple Witch doesn't give two shits about Ma'on or Oz. She thinks that she is God and wants to form Oz into her own likeness. She's a racist, a bully, an egotist, a narcissist, an idiot, and a sick fuck accused of assaulting women and men. She doesn't care what gender you are. If you've got genitalia, she'll assault them. Oh, and did I mention she's unqualified for the job?"

"Gee, Maria, why don't you tell me how you really feel!" I said, as I laughed and choked on the berry liquid from my juice box.

"This is serious, Dottie," said Maria, as she began to tear up. "Over 50 percent of Oz is supportive of her candidacy. Many of them are of the dominant religious sect, called the White Crusaders, and they believe the Wicked Witch of the West is Ma'on's anointed—sent to us by God to make us magnificent again. They have turned a blind eye and a deaf ear to the Purple Witch's blatant crimes and inhumanity. They are so desperate to bring back what they consider were the good old days when they were in control, they can't see how they're being slowly suffocated by an evil boa constrictor who is cutting off the blood supply to their hearts and brains.

"I have a confession to make, Dottie. I wasn't completely truthful with you when I told you my reasons for escorting you on this trip to the Emerald City. I used to work for Jonathan, and I am of the opinion that his political work led to his murder. He was the campaign manager for our current leader, President Adira, who can't seem to break through the smoke and mirrors of the Purple Witch. I didn't know Jonathan well, but I believed in his leadership and his vision for the true spirit of Oz which was supposed to be inclusive, caring, merciful, and loving. It was so in line with my great-grandpa's vision. Jonathan was trying to get us to embrace our history—the good, the bad, and the ugly —while getting back to our core values. This is a fact-finding trip for me as well as a personal one. I want to meet the Wizard, not only to get a brain, but I want to find out from him how he could love Ma'on and still support the Wicked Witch of the West. It just doesn't make sense."

"And your husband, was he or is he a GMOMA supporter?" I asked.

"One hundred percent true purple—ride or die! My inability to see eye-to-eye with him in his unholy alliance with the Wicked Witch of the West was the final straw that broke our marriage.

"We had an incident a while back when the Wicked Witch's loyalists stormed the Capitol building in Munchkinville to forcibly reinstall the Purple Wicked Witch. My ex-husband was the leader of the Tiger-Bear Boys who invaded the Capitol building, shat on the desks of our government leaders, tried to hang the Vice Witch, and murdered several of our Capitol police. Mortimer, my husband, was caught, tried, and convicted. He was carrying an enormous Ma'on sacred religious flag that he used to gouge the eyes of one of our police officers. My husband currently resides in the Emerald State Prison. Any hope we ever had of reconciling died on the Capitol building steps that morning when I saw his demon-possessed mug flash across Oz News Network as he screamed: *'The Purple Wicked Witch and Ma'on are one—long live the reign of the Wicked Witch of the West—Ma'on's anointed one!'*"

Maria and I rode in contemplative silence for a long time as we left the suburbs and moved rapidly through the countryside. Maria's sadness about a love lost to religious madness was palpable. Toe-Toe had climbed into my lap a while back to cuddle, and as I kissed her head, I whispered in her ear: "Well, Toe-Toe, I don't think this was the type of road trip your Dog Whisperer prescribed when he wanted us to relax and get to know each other. I have a feeling this is going to be one hell of a long bumpy ride!"

Chapter V

The Rescue of Dr. Stannum 'Tin' Chen

I had no idea how long we had been traveling, but if the rumblings in my stomach and Toe-Toe's incessant whining were any indications of anything, I figured it must be lunchtime. Plus, I had to pee—the perennial problem of women in our old age. I wish I had thought to ask Maria to procure me some leak-proof pads from the assisted-living wing of the hospital. I had the gorgeous skin and figure of a forty-year-old diva—emphatically proving that old generalization that "Black don't crack." But underneath the Spanx, the wigs, the fake eyelashes, and the acrylic nails was a road-weary, sixty-five-year-old woman staring down the bullet of old age with a bladder the size of a pea, and the inability to get from point A to point B without pissing her pants.

"I'm thinking we could all use a break," said Maria, as if she'd read my mind. "Why don't we pull off and park amid those large trees over there where we can't be easily seen from the road."

"Fine by me," I said. "My stomach's been growling for the last hour, and Toe-Toe and I are about to explode if we don't get a potty break soon."

Maria was able to find a giant oak tree with low-hanging branches that pretty much obscured our golf cart. She gathered one of the blankets and the box of food supplies and wandered down to a stream that was a few yards from our vehicle while Toe-Toe and I ducked behind a large azalea bush.

The boiled eggs and beef jerky followed by an apple juice box chaser tasted like the nectar of the gods. Even Toe-Toe gobbled up her dry dog food as if it were the finest chopped beef with an assortment of organic vegetables and a sprinkle of liver pâté. For a moment, we all forgot about our extraordinary mission and relaxed in the satiation of our humble feast and the warmth of the sun, as we fell into a somnolent state.

"*Grrrrr*," said Toe-Toe in a muted growl, which caused Maria and me to snap to attention.

"Do you hear something?" whispered Maria.

"No . . . wait a minute, yes!" I replied. "I hear groaning . . . under that large maple tree over there."

As the three of us cautiously crept toward the groaning sound, we were led to an old Chinese man who looked to be in his 80s. He had collapsed on the ground trying to crawl toward a cane that somehow had escaped his grasp and rolled down a slight embankment toward the stream.

"Thank you, kind folks," said the old man, as we approached. "I was hoping beyond hope that someone would come along and hear my cry for help. Would you please grab my cane so I can stand up?"

I helped the old man stand up and steady himself while Maria rescued his cane. We brushed the debris off of him as best we could, and then invited him to join us on our picnic blanket to compose himself.

"Where are my manners? Name is Dr. Stannum 'Tin' Chen. Ladies — 'tis a pleasure to meet you," said Dr. Chen, as he ravenously devoured a granola bar and an apple.

"Doctor? I'm a nurse—studying to be a medical doctor if I can ever get a brain," said Maria, as she shook hands with Dr. Chen.

"Oh, I'm not that kind of doctor," replied Dr. Chen. "Before I fully retired, I was the chair of the Department of Psychiatry and Behavioral Sciences at Oz University in Emerald City. I moved to this area of Oz after I finally stopped working at the university. I live just up the way, over that hill. I came down to the stream today to bring flowers to my wife's grave near the maple tree. This was her favorite spot on our property."

"I'm so sorry for your loss," I said. "How long has it been?"

"My Daiyu has been gone for just over a year now. But she was bedridden and suffered from dementia a year before that—she was barely able to communicate. So, technically, she's been gone for two years now. For a year she didn't remember that I was her husband. I miss her so much. Married sixty years, we were, and there isn't a day that goes by where I don't weep over the loss of her. She was the most beautiful and kindhearted woman ever created. God, I miss her so . . .."

Dr. Chen began to cry uncontrollably as Maria and I sat in an uncomfortable silence while trying to locate some tissues and search for comforting platitudes that we suspected would be as woefully unhelpful as a drop of water in a desert.

"My wife's death broke my heart," said Dr. Chen. "I didn't have much of a heart to begin with until she fell in love with me. Why she loved me, I will never know. I was nothing to write home about—always a shell of a man until I met Daiyu Wang. Her love enlarged my pathetic heart and made me whole."

"That's so sweet," Maria said, wiping a tear from her eye.

"I know what it means to lose someone you love whose love for you as a human being changes your life," I said, barely above a whisper as I thought about Jonathan.

"Tell us about your wife, Dr. Chen," said Maria.

For the longest time, the old man didn't say anything—just stared at the meandering stream. It was as if he were trying to conjure his wife to rise up out of the water to confirm to us what only his failing, loving memory could see.

"We met in high school," said Dr. Chen. "I was what the kids today call 'geeky'—a face full of acne, a gangly skeletal frame, and the posture of a drooping sunflower stalk on a hot summer Texas day. I was always looking down at my shoes and moving twice as fast as the other students around me. I suppose I did so in the hope of getting through life as quickly as possible without being seen by *anyone*. One day, I picked up my lunch tray in the cafeteria line and turned too fast without looking up and collided with the most beautiful brunette I had ever seen in my short life. There she was—this flawless vision of a girl—sprawled on the cafeteria floor with baked beans in her hair, meatloaf and gravy all over her beautiful yellow sweater and poodle skirt, and green beans sliding down her black and white saddle oxfords. I wished for the ground to open up and swallow me whole, but before I could utter the words, 'I'm so sorry,' Daiyu started laughing hysterically—laughing so hard that I did the unthinkable—*I laughed with her.*

"I tried to help her up from the floor, but the more I tried, the more she kept slipping and sliding on the baked beans and gravy, and pretty soon we were both on the floor laughing until we were crying from the absurdity of it all. That was the day we fell in love with each other and never stopped until death did us part.

"Daiyu—her name means black jade—loved me, warts and all. She said she loved my seriousness and intelligence. I loved her for her forgiving nature and her wicked sense of humor. Oh God . . .."

As Dr. Chen began to sob again, Maria said, "Back in the day, my mother's father set up grief support groups to help the surviving spouse adjust to their loved one's absence. Have any of those groups reached out to you?"

"Oh, they did more than reach out," said Dr. Chen as he bitterly threw his apple core into the stream with a strength that I didn't think was possible for such an old man. "They reached out, felt up, and sized me up.

"A group of old biddies was sent by that witch, Ernestine Early, to counsel me," hissed Dr. Chen. "Half of them rifled through Daiyu's jewels and dresses, while the other half put the moves on me and assessed my qualities as a potential husband. I'm eighty years old for God's sake! And my Daiyu wasn't cold in the grave yet when those harlequins were sizing me up for a wedding tux. Several of them left me business cards with their names, contact information, and personal notes on the back that said something tantamount to: 'If you need ANYTHING, and I do mean ANYTHING, don't hesitate to call!' *Sheesh!*

"My Daiyu may have broken my heart by dying, but those old crows chopped what was left of my heart into mincemeat and served it up in a vulture's pie. I can summarily announce that I no longer have a heart and I am all alone," said Dr. Chen as he burst into uncontrollable tears again.

While Maria and I gave the old man a couple of pathetic pat-pats on his shoulders and a few anemic "there-there's," Toe-Toe sprang into action and jumped into Dr. Chen's lap. She began to lick his face with the consoling, tender kisses of a holy spirit. An animal comfort I was learning that mainly a canine can give to the heart of a hurting human. *Cats can't do that. I know because I suddenly remembered that I owned a couple of Persian cats a while back. They were such debutantes that I could have taught them how to dial 911, and immediately afterwards had a stroke in front of them that caused me to writhe on the floor while gasping for air and screaming, "call 9-1-1." They would have ignored my pleas, turned their collective backs on me, and stuck their noses in the air, before they strutted down the street to go on about their feline business of being the coolest cats on the block. They were some cold bitches!* But I digress.

"Dr. Chen," I said. "We are on our way to see the Wizard to request that he give me a place to belong, and a brain for Maria. Since you seem to be aimless and alone, would you care to join us on our journey to the Emerald City to see if the Wizard can give you a new heart? At the very most, you might be pleasantly surprised what you end up with. At the very least, you'll get to go on a road trip with some boon companions."

"I'd love that," gushed Dr. Chen. "Just let me hobble back up to the house and fetch my fedora and some food supplies, and I'll be back in two shakes of a lamb's tail."

As Dr. Chen practically skipped up the hill, Maria and I began to pack up the souped-up golf cart to get back on the road. Dr. Chen returned before we even finished—dressed to the nines in a spiffy track suit with a matching fedora, a spotless pair of sneakers, and his cane. As our motley crew piled into the car, Toe-Toe promptly abandoned my lap for the lap of Dr. Chen. When Maria pressed the start button of our freedom-on-wheels, the old man excitedly declared: "We're off, my fellow travelers–off to see the Wizard, the wonderful Wizard of Oz!"

But nothing happened.

"Shit!" exclaimed Maria. "I knew I forgot something. Damn thing has run out of battery. I was in such a hurry to get us out of town that I forgot to check the charge level—it's completely dead. Once again, my brain has failed me when I needed it most."

"Well, now, don't despair," said a very disappointed Dr. Chen who refused to be thwarted now that a potential adventure was beckoning. "We'll just have to think of an alternative."

"Do you have a golf cart that we could borrow, Dr. Chen?" I asked. "These things seem to be ubiquitous in Oz."

"No, unfortunately. I mean, I own one, but it was stripped for parts a few nights back by some hooligans. They raided the entire neighborhood—like locusts swarming out of Hell. They left nothing but the carcass. Needless to say, it would be pretty useless to us in its current condition.

"I say! What if we hike the rest of the way?" suggested the slightly anxious Dr. Chen. He was not about to be daunted from going on a road trip with his first real company in over a year. He'd already grown fond of all of them in the brief half hour they'd eaten lunch together. Being with this motley crew was more soul-solidifying than anything he had experienced in a couple of years, and they hadn't even managed to move from under the tree where the golf cart was parked, yet.

"You all look in halfway decent shape," said Dr. Chen as he cast a dubious glance at me. "I have hiked these woods for years, and I know my way around the Emerald City like the back of my hand. I can be your guide to the city. Even with a cane, I can still make the trek."

"I have a cell phone with a compass and satellite reception, as well as an app that features seeing Oz via the scenic Yellow Brick Road," volunteered Maria. "Although we'll have to keep a low profile through certain regions that have travel warnings from OBI."

"OBI?" I mouthed.

"Oz Bureau of Investigations," replied Maria. "They send out weekly warnings about areas to avoid in Oz due to gang activity."

"Oh, OK . . .. Well, I have a 'can-do' attitude," I said, praying that my slightly chunky, old woman's body would not prove that statement to be a flat-out lie.

"Then let's do it!" shouted Dr. Chen, before any of us could change our minds.

On that note, probably three of the oddest companions in history set off into the woods to find our destinies in the hands of an all-knowing wizard.

Chapter VI

The Cowardly Pastor Leo Othniel

I don't remember who started our giddy revelry as we marched along arm in arm on our quest for answers, but we all remember who squelched it:

> *"We're off to see the Wizard,*
> *That grand ol' mighty Wizard.*
> *He IS the Man*
> *Who'll help our plans,*
> *The wise and awesome, Wiz . . ."*

"FREEZE!" commanded the disembodied thunderous voice that reverberated off the trunks of the bald cypress trees that engulfed us.

"WHO ARE YOU, AND WHAT ARE YOU DOING ON MY LAND?" roared the spine-numbing voice. "I HAVE A GUN, AND I'M NOT AFRAID TO USE IT. TAKE ONE MORE STEP, AND I'LL BLOW YOUR FUCKIN' BRAINS OUT, YOU . . . YOU DEMONS FROM HELL!"

We all instantly froze in mid-step, including Toe-Toe—doing our best impressions of a tableau of three humans and a dog frozen into a still-life painting.

"What should we do?" I whispered.

"Maybe we should go back the way we came, walking backward like when you come across a bear, doing so without turning our backs on him," whispered Dr. Chen. "They say it works for encounters with bears."

"*They say?*" I asked. "Who the hell is 'they?' I thought you were our hiker extraordinaire. When's the last time you ran into a bear who was speaking English and threatening your life with a gun?" I hissed hysterically.

"Or we could try to reason with him," whispered Maria. "What if we just explain our mission—that we were just passing through, and that we mean no harm . . .."

"SHUT UP! SHUT UP! I CAN'T HEAR MYSELF THINK ABOUT HOW I SHOULD DISPOSE OF THE LOT OF YOU, WITH ALL YOUR INCESSANT CHATTERING," said the over-modulated voice.

Before anyone knew what was happening, Toe-Toe jumped out of my arms and ran toward the voice in the woods. I ran after her but tripped and fell over my clunky magic shoes, and landed flat on my face. I heard Toe-Toe ferociously bark and growl, and then I heard the sound of the rifle go off, and the scary man's blood-curdling scream.

"TOE-TOE!" I yelled, as a six-foot tall, burly old Black man came bursting through the trees with a gun in one hand, a megaphone in the other, and Toe-Toe's teeth firmly sunk into his right ankle as if it were a T-bone steak.

"HELP! Get this monster off my leg," cried the old Black man. "Call your damn pit bull off of me before he kills me!"

I grabbed Toe-Toe as Dr. Chen started clobbering the man with his cane and Nurse Maria pummeled him with her overstuffed backpack.

To our great surprise, the big man collapsed to the ground and began to cry like an abandoned baby.

"Seriously, dude," I said with mounting irritation. "What are *you* blubbering about? You're the one who threatened us with a gun and tried to kill my dog, who by the way, is a girl and a Bichon Frisé."

"I was just trying to scare you off," he explained. "I...I wasn't going to shoot you. I wouldn't hurt a bug. I know I sound as if I have the voice of a ferocious lion—the megaphone really helps. But deep down inside, I'm a wimp—a proverbial coward."

"Well, a gun is no way to handle your fear of the unknown," I said. "We could have been your relatives or your neighbors. You could have killed us."

"I know, I know . . .." he replied. "I wasn't always this way—angry and volatile. I used to be a mighty, gentle, huggable bear for good, working for the church of Ma'on, until I got constantly bludgeoned and harassed by the likes of the Kiladah Tiger-Bear Boys."

"Nobody cares who you were before we met you, since this is our first time encountering you—the scary you, I might add," I said.

"Oh, I'm sorry," said the old Black man who suddenly seemed to shrink into a cuddly giant teddy bear that blubbered.

"My name is Pastor Leo Othniel—a shepherd with no sheep since my congregation got scattered to the four corners of Oz by the midnight raiders—the Kiladah Tiger-Bear Boys. Nobody good, kind, or gentle lives in these hills anymore, now that the Wicked Witch of the West's henchmen have been given full reign over the area. They sleep by day and terrorize by night carrying tiki torches and bearing enormous Purple Wicked Witch of the West territorial flags on F-150 souped-up golf carts when they storm our neighborhoods. The only way to survive anymore is by out-scaring them and out-shooting them. The human who can terrorize the crap out of another human in these parts wins the day."

"Wait a minute, I know you," said Maria. "You came to one of Jonathan Dubois's demonstrations once. I remember you because you seemed like such a kind and gentle soul, although rather braggadocious."

"I know. I'm ashamed to admit it now, but I was a real gasbag," said Pastor Leo. "Full of over-the-top fake bravado. I fooled myself and everyone around me into thinking I had real courage until it came time for the rubber to meet the road."

"No one ever knows if they have real courage until it's put to the test," said Dr. Chen.

"I lost my courage when I stood up against the Wicked Witch of The West's minions who tried to set up a hate club in Munchkinville under the guise that it was a history club," said Pastor Leo.

"At first, everyone went along with the new club because it seemed pretty innocuous—learning history about the war between the Northern and Southern parts of the Greater Land beyond Oz before it was formulated. We have a gazillion clubs in Oz. What was one more club?

"Slavery had proven to be a time of grave moral failure on the Greater Land's part but still some modern-day Ozians idealized that time period and wanted to revisit the concept of slavery as a good thing for Oz. It didn't matter that the Greater Land's slave masters were cruel and brutal—often breaking the mind, body, and souls of the enslaved who were their fellow human beings. In looking back, the ownership of another person resonated as a godly thing for some. Even though the Greater Land almost didn't survive that dance with evil, some Ozians wanted to rewrite that history and use it as a tutorial to reinstate a form of servitude for the ones that they deemed *others* in Oz. At one point, most of Oz agreed on why the war had been fought in the Greater Land: to dismantle slavery and build an equal and just society for all its citizens. Except fast forward a century or so, and the Wicked Witch of the West has repackaged that history as the 'good ol' days,' when people knew their place. Under the guise of a history club, her minions rewrote real history and labeled truth as lies and lies as truth.

"Jonathan was really the courageous one. He took them head-on and called them up to the higher values of the community, asking the residents to stand with him and fight to bring the liars' club down. So, I came prepared that night to speak. Even had a speech written. The Tiger-Bear Boys knew the people would listen to me as their pastor, so they threatened my life if I uttered a word in support of Jonathan's crusade to expose the bogus history club. They tried to terrorize Jonathan, but he told them off, in no uncertain terms, and continued to rally the community to reach toward their better selves and the higher cause that had drawn them all to Oz Heritage Settlement.

"The day I found out Jonathan was murdered—it destroyed me. I felt any ounce of courage I might have had leaked out of my pores. I never shared my speech at the meeting that night. I tore up the speech I had written to rise up against the Purple Wicked Witch, came back to these hills, and buried my head in the sand—hoping nobody would notice me. By that time, the Tiger-Bear Boys had run off all my congregation and confiscated their homes. Trust me. I hate myself for my lack of balls. I'd do anything to get back the courage I thought I had," wailed Pastor Leo.

We were all greatly moved by Pastor Leo's story because we all understood what it meant to lose a vital part of ourselves. Maria, Dr. Chen, and I talked amongst ourselves for a bit as Pastor Leo became lost in his own remorseful, torturous thoughts.

"Pastor Leo, we are on our way to see the Wizard to help me find where I belong, to help Maria get a brain that functions, and Dr. Chen to have his heart restored. Would you like to join us in our quest to see if the Wizard can give you courage?" I asked.

"And your vicious dog-who-is-not-a-pit-bull or a male," said Pastor Leo, "what is she going to the Wizard to get?"

"To rid herself of being a prissy-ass diva and get reprogrammed to become a ferocious German Shepherd or a Rottweiler who would take a chunk out of your ass the next time you scare us like you did," I jokingly said, as Maria and I fell out laughing at the shared vision of Toe-Toe as a Rottweiler dressed to the nines with a diamond collar, tiara, pink bows on each ear, and painted rainbow toes.

Not paying any attention to us, our preacher man began to do a Holy Ghost jig of gratitude. He performed a two-step, did a handstand, a backflip, and a cartwheel before we could calm him down enough to instruct him to go home and quickly grab a traveling bag with some eats, along with his gun, just in case. After he started jogging toward his home, we heard him singing at the top of his lungs in the most mellifluous baritone voice I'd ever heard before then or since: "GLORY, HALLELUJAH! MA'ON IS AN AWESOME GOD, FOR TRULY HE HAS SAVED MY SORRY BEHIND THIS DAY!"

Too bad the Wizard couldn't have airdropped some courage on us all—right that very afternoon—because we were surely going to need it come sundown.

CHAPTER VII

Journey to Emerald City

Adding Pastor Leo to the group proved to be a good call. Once he got over his fear, he was a very relaxed and jovial companion, even if he was an incessant talker.

"I loved, loved, loved being a pastor," said Pastor Leo, as we made our way through the woods, always keeping the Yellow Brick Road in sight. "I loved my parishioners like they were my blood relatives. I loved being a part of their lives—being there when they needed a helping hand through disappointment and grief. Loved performing their weddings, baptisms, and the liturgy. Ever since I can recall, I wanted to help people get out of their own way and just become their most authentic selves—as God created them to be. Unfortunately, I have found that most people undershoot their potential because they get hung up on the minutiae of everyday life while many others overshoot their ability to just be because they misinterpret their craven desires as being God's will.

"I had a parishioner once who was a very pious man who just wanted to obey Ma'on—no more, no less. When you hear this story, you're going to think he was mentally ill, but I assure you he was not. Looking back on the situation, he might have been a little simple, but he just wanted to make sure that everything he did complied with his most holy God, as he understood it so that he could live a blessed life. He figured he only had one life to live and didn't want to mess it up. The problem was he thought that being obedient to God was in the external manifestations of rituals and fundamentalist do's and don'ts—the 'God will strike me dead,' kind of thing—and he demanded things of himself that no God of truth would ask of their followers.

"One day his wife called me, almost out of her mind with agitation. Said her husband refused to put any clothes on. Said he'd been carrying on like that for weeks now. I immediately went looking for him, and I found him walking around our town square absolutely butt naked.

"I said, 'Joe, why are you out here in the freezing cold with no clothes on?' You know what he said to me? 'I'm waiting for Ma'on to tell me what kind of weather we're going to have today so I know whether to put on shorts and a T-shirt or cargo pants and a long-sleeve hoodie. Why waste time? I figured I'd cut to the chase and go straight to the horse's mouth.'

"'Well Joe,' I said after some thought. 'The way I see it is when Ma'on made you, he also inspired someone to invent the Weather Channel. Now Ma'on ain't gonna do for you what you can do for yourself. The truth is, you'll end up freezing your nuts off before you hear a directive from heaven that proclaims, 'JOE, GET THY SKINNY ASS INTO A PAIR OF LONG PANTS AND A SWEATER BECAUSE I'M GOING TO DUMP A BUTT-LOAD OF SNOW ON YOUR TOWN TODAY—THUS, SAITH MA'ON!' So, for the sake of us all —especially your lovely wife—would you please download the weather app on your phone, and let us all go about our day without having to take a gander at your noodle and plums, cause ain't nobody got time for this today?'

"You know what? We never had any more trouble with him getting dressed after that. Although it gave me plenty of belly laughs whenever I thought of our conversation. Unfortunately, I could no longer look at him from the pulpit or I'd keel over in laughter. In the end, poor Joe didn't need a sermon, he just needed a little dose of common sense. And I truly loved him for his childlike faith.

"The worst parishioners—the ones who were a constant pain in my ass—were the know-it-alls. They were the ones who thought they sat at the right hand of God, had life all figured out, and were under the mandate from God to tell everyone else how to live. I could never get through to those hard-ass busybodies, and they caused me many sleepless nights."

"I left the church—no, *the church left me*—a long time ago," mused Maria, as she thought about poor Joe. "Once the church started getting into politics, especially with the Purple Wicked Witch of the West, I exited stage left. Another reason I want to meet the Wizard is that I have a gazillion questions as to why he's seemingly not spoken out against the Purple One. In fact, by his actions, the Wizard seems to be in bed with the Purple Wicked Witch."

"Well, at the end of the day," said Pastor Leo, "my church left me too. Most of them got seduced by the wealth of the Emerald City Cathedral's mega church and its 'name it and claim it doctrine.' Others just drifted away because they weren't really interested in community and serving other human beings who had less than they did. After all, they'd moved to Oz to spend the rest of their days playing golf, drinking margaritas, and having unprotected sex—making us the STD champions of all the fifty-five-plus communities, by the way. I heard that a few of them might have even joined the Tiger-Bear Boys—a weird military cult whose members spend their days playing old man soldiers and their nights stealing golf carts to sell on the black market."

"It's getting near the end of the day," cautioned Dr. Chen. "I think it would be wise to find some shelter before nightfall. There should be small caves up on the ridge just beyond the curve in the road. I suggest we camp there tonight."

We were all in agreement, especially me because I had multiple blisters from the Wicked Witch of the East's magic clogs. Unfortunately, no matter how hard I tried to remove her shoes, they would not budge.

As we located an acceptable cave and began to rummage through our various backpacks to make a meal, we saw a sudden blaze of torches light up the sky down the hill from our encampment. Pastor Leo cautioned us to be quiet as we crept down the incline to see what was going on. Just as we rounded a boulder that had obscured our view, we saw a mass of old White men dressed in costumes that consisted of the bottom half of a bear's hide attached by suspenders to their shoulders with the top half of the costume made of striped yellow and black furry material which covered their upper bodies and heads. Their faces were covered with tiger masks. Gigantic banners draped the campsite with slogans that said: *To be eliminated upon the return of the Purple Wicked Witch of the West—Niggers, Fags, Drag Queens, Kikes, Beaners, Whores, All Dogs except Pit Bulls and Doberman Pinschers, Cats—TBD.* There looked to be about 100 or so of them, and they all carried tiki torches while they stumbled in a drunken, hypnotic trance around a massive bonfire chanting slogans of hate:

> *"Jews will not replace us;*
> *Blacks won't overtake us,*
> *Whites will rule the day,*
> *Terror is our way!"*

"Retreat, retreat, retreat!" whispered Pastor Joe. "Not to overstate the obvious, but we need to get as far away from here as possible, and I don't think the cave is far enough."

"Agreed," said Dr. Chen. "If my memory serves me right, there is a very large old abandoned greenhouse about a mile up on the upper path, but we won't be able to use our flashlights. Hold on to each other's waistbands and belts so we don't get separated in the dark, and for Ma'on's sake, don't make a sound! In fact, try not to even breathe."

I honestly don't know how we made it to the ridge. But sure enough, we were able to locate what seemed like an abandoned greenhouse at first.

Except it wasn't.

We blew past the "KEEP OUT OR YOU WILL BE SHOT" sign, pried open the door, and stumbled into an immense space filled with all manner of large, colorful hibiscus trees around the perimeter, scads of golf cart parts piled up on each other formed the next ring, and in the pot-of-gold middle, we discovered rows and rows and rows of marijuana plants.

I don't remember who bit the dust first, I just know that I was the last man standing, so to speak, as my head started swimming and I vomited all over Toe-Toe. It was when I heard Pastor Leo croak out, "ABORT, ABORT, it's a booby trap"—that's when I knew we were toast.

Chapter VIII

The Enchanting Hibiscus Plants and the What Not Chop Shop

Maybe someday Toe-Toe will be able to tell us how she saved our lives from the poisonous gas trap set by the Tiger-Bear Boys, but until then, I'll simply have to guess by putting two and two together.

I came to my senses first because of the excruciating pain that broke through my fog and brought me back to life enough to realize that I needed to crawl my way back out of the greenhouse. The source of the pain and the effusive blood pouring from my ankle was Toe-Toe. She had practically ripped a hole in my ankle to get me to wake up. After I stumbled out of the poison gas that was being pumped in through the overhead vents, I watched Toe-Toe through my blurred vision as she barked incessantly while running back and forth between me and the entrance to the greenhouse. It quickly dawned on me that I had to pull the others out of our entrapment before they died from the poison gas.

I spotted a used towel on the ground and soaked it in water from a rain barrel sitting off to the corner of the building and tied it around my nose and mouth. There were several wheelbarrows off to the left and with all the strength I could muster, Toe-Toe and I double-teamed the rescue: she bit ankles and barked in ears as I plopped the others—one by one—into wheelbarrows and pushed them out into the fresh air.

It couldn't have been more than thirty minutes or so, but it seemed like hours as all of us reacted to the poisoning—coupled with relief—and vomited or clutched our hearts as it felt like we were having heart attacks. We collectively moaned in agony from the life-saving bites of our hero, Toe-Toe.

Despite it all, Pastor Leo soon whipped us into shape. He became our general, determined to get us—his troops—out of the danger zone. He first demanded we shut up, sit up, take long, deep breaths, and fill our lungs with fresh air. Then he commanded Maria to bandage our ankles with her first aid kit and sent Dr. Chen to find a golf cart we could commandeer. I was useless to him because all I could do was sob hysterically and rock back and forth as I practically crushed Toe-Toe to death against my chest as I demonstrated my sheer gratitude and over-whelming love for this courageously smart puppy.

"Well, well, well," said Pastor Leo as he heaved a sigh of relief. "Everybody OK?

"Looks like our potential deathtrap turned out to be the central headquarters for the Tiger-Bear Boys chop shop operation. It appears the recent run on stolen and stripped golf carts could all be traced back to this greenhouse. Their legitimate business is selling hibiscus plants to the copious retirees in Oz—a lucrative business since the plants are in high demand throughout Oz. But they couldn't stop there, it seems. Looks like the good ol' boys are running drugs as well, and I think the reason we didn't get caught tonight is because they have gotten high on their own supply as they're egging each other on to foment their next tiki torch march to terrorize the citizens of Oz."

Whatever the case was in that evil waystation, we all hopped up and down with overwhelming joy on each of our one unbitten leg when Dr. Chen pulled up in a souped-up, four-seater Ferrari golf cart that he had found tucked up under a tarp behind the building. He also confirmed our suspicions of the gas poisoning. When he rummaged around for an escape vehicle, he saw several discarded containers with skull-and-crossbones decals marked: "DANGER!" We surmised that there must have been some type of tripwire on the door which activated the booby trap. I suppose we'll never know exactly what we stumbled into, but we didn't care—we just wanted to get as far away from our deathtrap as possible.

As we peeled out of the seventh circle of *Dante's Inferno* and made our way onto the Yellow Brick Road—speeding toward Emerald City—I whispered a prayer of thanksgiving to the universe. I also fired off a missive to Jonathan in the Great Beyond as I smothered Toe-Toe with copious kisses: "JONATHAN, DARLIN,' I *LOVE* OUR PUFFBALL OF A DOG!"

CHAPTER IX

The Emerald Glass Cathedral of Oz

We sped along the Yellow Brick Road in the contemplative silence of a group of people who had suffered a collective brush with death and knew that no words we could possibly utter would bring comfort to assuage the terror that still resonated within us.

One by one we drifted off to sleep, except for Dr. Chen who was driving. The last glimpse I had of his face before I dozed off was the locked-jaw determination of a man who had already suffered one loss of someone he loved, and he was not about to lose his new companions—his new found family.

It was the scent of Texas mountain laurel assaulting my nostrils that woke me up, and the glare of the rising sun that completed the wake-up call for us all. Suddenly our nostrils were overwhelmed with the intoxicating smells of a dozen perfume bottles.

"Do you smell that?" I asked as I pointed to the various flowers along the road. "Oh my God! See those yellow and violet flowers? Those are butterfly bushes. Those clusters over there are sweet olives, and *ooh, ooh, ooh,* here comes my favorite on the left: *gardenias!* Look on your right. There are banana shrubs! Can you smell the banana with just a hint of ripe cantaloupe? Oh, my God, look at the profusion of petunias, dianthuses, jonquils, and poppies—this is a highway to Heaven," I exclaimed as I clapped my hands enraptured by the beautiful floral scene unfolding before us.

"Well, it looks like someone got her memory back, Dottie," said Maria. "At least the gardener part."

"Yeah . . . I guess so. It's coming back in a flood. I *love* growing flowers. They bring me such peace and joy. It's fabulous! Of all my memories to come back so quickly, my gardening ones are the most precious because there is nothing negative about them."

We were all overwhelmed by the beauty surrounding us. As we got lost in my docent revelations of every single flower, shrub, and tree we passed, houses painted green, enclosed by fences painted green, began to dot the landscape.

"Oh my," said an awestruck Maria. "Look at that green glow up ahead. It's getting brighter and brighter the closer we move toward it. What do you think it is?"

At that very moment, the morning haze departed and a blast of sunlight spread its rays upon a glorious Emerald Glass Cathedral, which took up the entire skyline. We were so stunned and gobsmacked by its magnitude that we almost crashed into the enormous door in the gigantic wall that marked the end of the Yellow Brick Road. Not only was the door in the wall the largest I'd ever seen, but it was framed in an abundant trim of purple wisteria and it smelled divine.

Above the top of the gigantic door was a giant bell with a pull cord that only Pastor Leo was tall enough to reach. He promptly pulled on it with all his might which caused a very disturbing racket that crudely juxtaposed the beautiful tranquility we had experienced for the past fifteen minutes.

There was no answer.

"You mean to tell me we've come all this way, and nobody's home?" said a very frustrated Maria.

"Try again," I demanded. "This place looks much too big for there not to be anybody home. I can't see the end of this wall, either to my left or to my right. This is the barrier of a metropolis. There has to be a small army guarding this place."

Just as Pastor Leo started to pull the rope again, the green head of a hirsute, pudgy old man popped his head through an oval opening above the door and bellowed out: "WHO'S MAKING ALL THAT RACKET? WHAT DO YOU WANT?"

"We've come to see the Wizard," said Maria.

"THERE IS NO ONE HERE BY THE NAME OF 'THE WIZARD,'" replied the gatekeeper looking down on us from his oval hole in the wall from above. "HE DROPPED THAT MONIKER LAST SEASON. HE IS NOW REFERRED TO AS THE 'RIGHT REVEREND EMERALD, THE DIVINE!' IF YOU WERE FROM AROUND THESE PARTS, YOU'D KNOW THAT!"

"OK," I said, trying not to lose my patience. "Sorry, sorry, slip of the tongue. *Please* forgive us; we've traveled a long way in order to get his advice on some urgent matters. We're exhausted and extremely hungry. Please let us in; we'd like to see the Right Reverend Emerald, the Divine."

"IS HE EXPECTING YOU?" barked the gatekeeper.

"Now, you listen here, Mister," said an apoplectic Dr. Chen as he shook his cane up at the gatekeeper. "I am Dr. Stannum Chen. I realize it was a long time ago, but I was the chair of the Department of Psychiatry and Behavioral Sciences at Oz University. That should count for something. My family and I are at our wits end. We were told that the Emerald City Cathedral was a welcoming place and that the Right Reverend Emerald, the Divine guards the truth of Oz. So, we are in no mood for bullshit. Open this gate and let us in because if you don't, I'll find a way to break down this door and pummel you to smithereens. Have I made myself clear?"

"ALL RIGHT, ALL RIGHT—NO NEED TO GET VIOLENT! HOLD YOUR HORSES."

After what seemed to be an eternity, a door about ten feet tall, eight feet wide, and more than twenty tons, began to slowly open and come abruptly to a full stop when it was perpendicular to the wall. As if by magic, a three-foot tall, swarthy, bearded, rotund man in a green military uniform, wearing green glasses walked out to greet us.

"Welcome to Emerald City—the birthplace of the House of Ma'on, affectionately known as the House of Oz," said the little man magnanimously in a diminutive voice. "My name is Otto, the gatekeeper. Before you cross the threshold of this entryway, you must put on these green sunglasses which I will lock on the back of your heads. As long as you are in Oz, you must never remove them. Is that clear?"

"Why?" asked Maria. "What is the purpose of these glasses?"

"Well, uh . . . uh," stammered the gatekeeper. "If you don't wear the green glasses, the overwhelming brightness of the city will blind you."

"That's a bullshit answer, if I ever heard one," whispered Pastor Leo. "Dr. Chen, do you remember this nonsense rule when you lived here?"

"No," replied Dr. Chen. "Of course, there was no Wizard and no cathedral when I went to school here and worked at the university. The city also wasn't this large. There's probably been a lot of changes since my time."

"Just do it," I said. "The sooner we comply the sooner we'll get an audience with the Wizard."

Once our green glasses were secured, the gatekeeper placed an open palm on a picture screen to the right of a slightly smaller door that was behind him. When the interior door opened, a bustling marketplace was revealed—all in green. Men and women, children and pets, and vendors hawking their wares with everything from flowers, meats and vegetables, to local art. Except for all the people being the color green, everyone seemed very happy, content, and prosperous.

When we arrived at the center of the marketplace, we were met by a young woman driving a six-seater golf cart, who the gatekeeper introduced as our tour guide and personal assistant: Tiffany.

"How's everybody doing today?" chirped Tiffany. A young green-haired girl, dressed in green from head to toe and sporting the demeanor of an overeager cheerleader, said, "I understand you're here to see the Right Reverend Emerald, the Divine. Before you do that, RRED, as we locals affectionately call him, has instructed me to show you around the cathedral—the most breathtaking building in Oz—and then get you checked into our guest suites to freshen up before the special evening church service."

"Excuse me, Miss," I said. "I don't mean to be rude, and I'm sure the Emerald City Cathedral is just exquisite, but can we cut to the chase and go straight to see the Wizard?"

"Oh no," replied Tiffany, "I'm afraid not. RRED is deep in prayer and preparation for the special service tonight. He never lets anyone interrupt his communication with Ma'on before a church service. You'll have to wait until afterwards. I believe you're scheduled for an audience with RRED at 8pm sharp—thirty minutes after the close. I will personally escort you to RRED himself."

On that note, and with no other recourse, we soon plodded behind Tiffany as she chirped on and on about how the cathedral was the largest emerald glass structure in the world measuring around 90,000 square-feet. It could seat 10,000 people at a time with its 4,000 pews on the main floor and six balconies. The cathedral was shaped like a five-pointed star and it was longer than two football fields. It also featured more than 20,000 panes of glass. Miss Tiffany was quick to point out that according to Ozipedia, the church houses "one of the largest pipe organs in the world."

"During the Christmas season," prattled Tour Guide Tiffany, (as Maria and Dr. Chen made 'shoot me now' gestures with their fingers against their temples), "there isn't a church in the world that can top our Christmas pageant. It features 1,000 singers, a 400-piece orchestra, live camels and horses, and dozens of our skinnier people flying over the congregation on overhead cables. I've been a flying angel for three years in a row—I can't begin to express what an honor it is!"

Just when I was about to swat Miss Tiffany to the moon, we arrived on the sixth floor of the cathedral where our suites were housed.

"Pastor Leo and Dr. Chen," directed Miss Tiffany, "you'll take the two-bedroom suite on my left. Maria and Dorothy, you'll take the two-bedroom suite on my right. While you all get settled in, I'll take Madame Toe-Toe with me to the groomers. Dinner will be brought to you by room service and I'll return at 5:45 p.m. to escort you to be a part of the greatest show on Earth. Ta-ta for now!"

With that, Miss Tiffany vanished around the corner of the hallway carrying my precious Toe-Toe whose green glasses were perched on top of her dirty, tangled, frazzled head in such a way that she looked like a crazed tarsier from Indonesia. She stretched out her two front paws toward me, and I swear I heard her barks say, *"H-e-l-p me, Mommy! This chirpy hoot owl is going to kill me!"*

CHAPTER X

The Right Reverend Emerald, the Divine

I can't remember if I was a diva before landing in Oz, but my reaction to being pampered to the utmost degree would probably lean heavily to that conclusion.

My Emerald City Cathedral suite had a butler who drew my bath with an obscene amount of bubbles, gave me a massage, supplied me with an expensive new curly wig, provided me with a rack of gorgeous Sunday-go-to-meeting clothes (albeit all in green), polished my magic shoes while still on my feet because even he couldn't remove them no matter how hard he tried, and served me a meal of a two-inch ribeye steak, mashed potatoes, and perfectly creamed spinach, topped off with a mouth-watering Cabernet Sauvignon. Maria had *suffered* the same pampering, and when we came together—dressed to the nines in our green velvet and satin gowns—we joined hands and giddily jumped up and down like two teenagers going to our senior prom.

"Can you believe the opulence of this place?" I asked Maria. "Wasn't that chocolate mousse unbelievable?! It seems as if all you have to do is name it, and you get to claim it here. *OMG!* I wonder how the boys are faring?"

Just at that moment, the suite doorbell rang.

"Come in—door's open," Maria and I chimed in unison. In walked two Dapper Dans. Pastor Leo had on a Dolce & Gabbana suit, with an open shirt, Italian leather shoes, and a gold Rolex watch—a gift from the Right Reverend Emerald, the Divine. Dr. Chen sported a three-piece Emporio Armani suit, replete with a gorgeous silk tie and matching pocket square. He had turned down the gift of the Rolex in exchange for a new cane—hand carved—and a Bruno Capelo fedora with a feather in the brim.

We thought we were all that and a bag of chips until Tour Guide Tiffany returned Toe-Toe to us. Our restoration didn't have anything on Toe-Toe! Babygirl had been shampooed, blow-dried, trimmed, and coiffed. Her head, body, and tail were three perfectly geometrical green snowballs, with a small snowball of hair at the end of each of her shaved legs—topped off by green painted toenails. Each puffball ear was topped with a green bow, and her neck sported an emerald Swarovski collar. Haughty-as-hell Toe-Toe pranced in on her toes, and when I managed to catch her eye and mouthed the words, *"I can handle anything about your new look except you back up on your tippy toes, Babygirl. Get back down on all fours,"* I swear she gave me the side-eye before complying.

And so, this was how we descended to the vestibule of the Emerald Cathedral as if we were entering a high-rollers casino in Vegas looking like a senior citizen Mod Squad along with their diva mascot. Tiffany marched us through a private door into the sanctuary of the cathedral and escorted us down to the VIP section in the second row of the middle orchestra.

As I discovered later, they would be the perfect seats to have our minds pickled and our souls slimed.

Thousands of mostly old White people were standing, clapping, and singing in unison with the worship team on stage that consisted of ten singers, a full band, and a dozen female dancers in green long-sleeve turtlenecks and long satin skirts. The sound of thousands of people singing in unison was cacophonous although oddly transcendent. The dancers seemed like marionettes, only lifting their arms and legs so far off the ground, as if moving other parts of their bodies, in their sacrificial dance of praise to the God Ma'on, would offend his sensibilities if he saw a little leg.

At the end of the worship service, a deacon came to the podium and called up two audience members to give their testimonies. "Tell everybody your name, your age, and what you named and claimed from Ma'on this week. Most importantly, tell us what you got."

"Hi everybody," said an elderly woman. "My name is Mabel Henderson, I'm sixty-five years old. I'm the proud grandmother of four grandkids, and I live over in Winkie Country. I named a mink fur coat like I saw on one of the rich ladies in Emerald City, and you know what? I GOT IT Y'ALL! I named it and claimed it! Always wanted one of those fine fur coats. Next time I'm gonna pray for a designer bag to go with it!"

"I saw that coat, Mabel," someone shouted from the audience. "Ain't no mink, it's made of rabbit. Looks like you better ratchet up your faith, girl."

Several members in the audience tittered, and the deacon scolded them, "Just 'cause your faith ain't large enough to claim a fur coat— mink or otherwise—doesn't mean you got the right to judge Mabel. Thank you, Mabel, dear.

"Next testimonial is from Amos Patterson. Tell us your name-it-and-claim-it story," said the deacon.

"Well, as you heard, my name is Amos. I'm seventy-five years old, and since there's not much I don't have on this Earth, I named and claimed a gorgeous 590-foot-long luxury yacht to be parked in my private marina behind my heavenly mansion as my reward when I pass on to glory. For obvious reasons, I can't claim it yet 'cause I ain't dead yet. But I'm believin' Ma'on will keep his promise. 'Ask and you shall receive,' as the Good Book says! Ma'on didn't say *when* I'd receive it though after I go on to Glory."

"AMEN!" shouted the congregation.

"THAT'S ALL RIGHT, BROTHER!" shouted a man from the first-level balcony, "YOU JUST KEEP THE FAITH—MA'ON WILL REWARD YOU!"

"Glory be to God; yes, he will," chimed the bleached blond woman in front of me.

"Good on you, Amos," said the deacon. "I guess we'll all have to wait until we get to glory to see you claim your earthly desire. Let's give these two believin' souls a hearty round of applause."

"Are you shittin' me?" whispered Pastor Leo to me. "Let me see if I got this straight: A human being is supposedly offered the opportunity to co-exist in an eternal realm with a heavenly being—the God who created the universe and all the universes still unheard of—and the best they can do is lust after earthly possessions that they lusted after on Earth? I don't know what I find more appalling—the failure of imagination or the sheer wickedness of this creepy false doctrine."

"*Shhhhh!*" scolded the woman in front of us.

Poor bamboozled Amos took his seat and the deacon announced that the tithes and offerings would be collected at this point. The assistant pastor skipped to the podium.

"Evening, y'all. To all the visitors with us today, I am Reverend Two-Step," said the Wizard's right-hand man. "We now come to the best and most important part of the service. A chance for you to participate in the work of God. Time for y'all to cough up the shekels—to give back to the God who has been so good to you. And I don't mean your leftovers after you've paid your bills, bought your groceries, and made your child support. I mean your first fruits *before* you pay anything else if you want to be properly blessed by Ma'on.

"We've been checking the books, by the way, and some of y'all have fallen behind in your financial obligations to Ma'on. Our God has told us that our Emerald City Cathedral—his house—is in need of expansion and more glorification. But we can't obey God's command to expand until you stick to the plan—10 percent, 20 percent, 30 percent or more. Don't you know you can't outgive God! The more you sow, the more you'll reap. Amen? *A-a-a-men!*"

"Goddamnit!" exclaimed Pastor Leo, who began pounding his fist against his head in complete frustration at the heresy being proclaimed.

"Blasphemer," hissed the woman sitting next to me as she leaned over to swat at Pastor Leo with her holy book.

Sensing the righteous anger in Pastor Leo that was quickly erupting into a torrent of expletives, I moved up and placed myself like a bookmark in between them, before he attempted to pummel that silly old woman with his words. I put on a saccharine smile and offered Miss Self-Righteous a hand full of green gummy bears that I'd swiped from my suite. As I emptied the candy from my purse into the lap of the holy roller, I sweetly patted her hand and said, "There, there, my sister, you must forgive him—he just a little bit touched in the head in his old age," all the while making the universal sign with my finger of someone who has dementia.

"He's got the Tourette's on top of everything else, you know. Can't help himself. Goes off at the drop of a dime. Being the good, holy woman you are, I'm sure you understand the burden I bear being his sister, and all."

That charade, added to the gummy bears, shut the aggrieved woman up. I then turned to Pastor Leo and gave him one of my Toe-Toe skank eyes that wordlessly screamed, "ENOUGH! FOCUS!" in the hopes that would put an end to him getting riled up.

"Congregation, visitors, and the like, the person who you all came here tonight to see and be blessed by," announced Reverend Two-step. "Now without further ado, *h-e-r-e's* the Right Reverend Emerald, THE DIVINE!"

The crowd jumped to its feet with thunderous applause as the gigantic string section of the orchestra played the opening of *Thunderous* by Victor López, and the flood lights dramatically tilted toward the top of the cathedral. The audience gasped in ecstasy as a thin, wiry man dressed in a Hugo Boss suit ensemble with slicked-back black hair, a sprayed-on golden tan, and a billowing cape attached to his shoulder pads descended from the ceiling. He wore diamond rings on his pinkies, a Rolex diamond watch on his wrist, and carried a diamond-encrusted holy book in his right hand. The Wizard; the Right Reverend Emerald, the Divine; RRED; or whatever name he chose to go by, spread his arms and blessed his congregation with a thrice-bleached broad smile, and took a grand bow.

"Well, well, well," said Pastor Leo with deep scorn and rather loudly, "the flim-flam man has finally arrived, y'all. Hold on to your credit cards, your checkbooks, and your wives!" At which point, the woman in front of us leaned back and yelled, "HEATHEN, REPROBATE!"—took a broad swing—and smacked Pastor Leo repeatedly upside his head with her holy book until I saw tears in his eyes. I'm pretty sure *he saw stars*.

Chapter XI

The Flim-Flam Man Underscores His Plans

The Wizard was too engulfed in soaking up the glory from the congregation to notice the pew rage happening in front of him between one of his female parishioners and Pastor Leo. Fortunately, Pastor Leo restrained himself and never lifted a finger toward his assailant. At my urging, Dr. Chen traded seats with Pastor Leo, which seemed to satisfy the angry woman because she returned her adoring gaze to the Right Reverend Emerald, the Divine, and settled down.

"Evening, my sheep," said the Right Rev. "How's everybody doing tonight?"

"GREAT, PASTOR!" shouted the congregation.

"That's just wonderful because I have a really special message for you tonight. But first, let me tell you about our new merch on sale at the display booth in the lobby for the Purple Wicked Witch of the West's presidential campaign. Many of you already have the purple ball caps that say 'Purple 2024' and the T-shirts that say 'Ma'on is my God, but Purple is my President.' *Hallelujah!*

"Today, Purple's campaign delivered to us leatherbound holy books with the inscription, 'God Bless Oz.' Along with the Holy Scriptures inside, you'll find the full text of the Oz Constitution and lyrics to that glorious patriotic song, *This Land is Oz Land*—written by our very own Pastor Two-step.

"Now that holy book is perfectly fine if you want a great bargain at $69.99. However, if you want to join the bling patrol with your favorite Rev, Sister Amanda has set up shop right next to the holy book kiosk and will swag your book to the hilt with her green rhinestones and glue gun.

"What does the color green represent, my people?"

"MONEY!" shouted the congregation.

"What can't we get enough of in Oz?" prompted the Wizard.

"MONEY, MONEY, MONEY," chanted the parishioners in unison.

"All right, all right, all right!" exclaimed the cheerleader man of Ma'on.

As two twentysomething, gorgeous blond women unhooked the cape from the Rev's shoulders—indicating it was time to get *really* serious—the congregation settled down and took out their notepads, ready to capture every syllable of the Wizard's sermon.

In a serpentine conspiratorial voice, the Rev whispered into the microphone: "Don't tell anybody, but we're into Holy Crusaderism— what our critics call 'White Ma'on Nationalism.'"

The audience chuckled and bowed their heads in unison as if on cue by a conductor directing them to do so with a baton.

"Heavenly Ma'on," prayed the Rev, "you told me today that my sermon need not be long; my sermon just needs to remind your people about the obligation we have to put the right witch in office come Election Day. God, you told me to tell the people that the Purple Wicked Witch of the West was sent here by you to fulfill our crusader agenda of taking back this land for your glory, which is why we need to reelect Purple. Ma'on, you created this land, and you said to remind the people how Purple has almost fulfilled our manifesto, she just needs a limitless reign to fulfill the rest. Thank you, God. In your name, I declare all these truths. Amen? *Amen!*"

Two jumbotron screens on each side of the cathedral came to life on the second 'amen,' and the title of the Rev's sermon emerged: *Emerald City Cathedral's Ten Summits of Domination: Taking Oz Back for Ma'on—One Summit at a Time.*

I dozed in and out while the Rev droned on and on about the proposed domination of all of Oz via the *Ten Summits*—"strongholds to rule the land"—he called them. But I snapped to attention when a list of the Summits of Control rolled onto the screens: *Family, Sexuality, Religion, Education, Media, Entertainment, Business, Government, Women's Bodies, and Independent Thought.*

Suddenly the sermon ended, as if the Wizard had run out of gas, and he shouted: "LET IT BE KNOWN ACROSS THE LAND: THOSE WHO WILL NOT CONFORM AND OBEY MA'ON'S RIGHT-EOUS TENETS WILL BE ELIMINATED AND/OR REMOVED FROM THE WONDERFUL LAND OF OZ!"

An earsplitting roar of approval rose out of the congregation as thousands of people simultaneously jumped to their feet and danced in place with jubilation at the prospect of Oz completely controlled—from hearth to the halls of government—by the groupthink of the self-righteous.

The organist began to play the hymn, *Just as I Am*, while the Right Reverend conducted an altar call. A summons to all the sinners and unfaithful in the auditorium to come forth and repent of their sins so that they could go back out into Oz and live the unadulterated name-it-and-claim-it holy life of the sanctified—lives controlled by the few who demanded obeisance from the many to their way of life—no exceptions to the rule.

I don't know how long we sat there without moving or speaking as hordes of enthusiastic people on a mission from God cleared out of the auditorium. Dr. Chen looked bemused—peering into each of our faces in disbelief. Maria appeared terribly sad and uncomfortable—as if she'd rather be anyplace else but here in the "House of God." Pastor Leo was visibly heartbroken and angry—as though he listened to the death knell of his faith and his entire life's work.

I began to remember something else about my former life: I had once been a believer in the God of my realm and his church until my House of God, the equivalent of their House of Oz, betrayed me by a similar spirit of capitulation to the idolatry of mammon and a vile leader.

And I was undone.

Chapter XII

The Search for the
Purple Wicked Witch of the West

"The Right Reverend Emerald, the Divine, will see you now," said Tiffany when she came to collect us from the empty sanctuary after the service.

"Wait," said Pastor Leo, while he stripped the Rolex off of his wrist. He stared at it for a hot Emerald City minute, as if he'd removed a poisonous snake from his arm. "I think we all should go back to the suite and change clothes. This shit is a trap—it clouds the mind and the spirit. I need to clear my head." As we all nodded in agreement, Pastor Leo said, "Tiffany, please bring us the clothes we traveled to Emerald City in."

"But . . . there's no time for that now," protested Tiffany. "RRED is waiting for you; you can't keep him waiting. Besides, I sent your clothes to be laundered, and I don't think they've returned yet. I'll tell you what, you can change clothes . . ."

"*NOW*, TIFFANY! WE'LL TAKE OUR CLOTHES AS IS!" roared Pastor Leo.

Chirpy Tiffany ran like a rabbit being chased by a starving fox and managed to rustle up our old clothes. They had not been washed yet, but they smelled like the sweetest-smelling roses compared to the rotting stench of the finery the Wizard had tried to seduce us with.

Toe-Toe was reluctant to let go of her Swarovski necklace though. I counteracted with a mind meld that silently said, *"I'm your mother, and you'll obey me because I say so, or your ass is grass."* She begrudgingly let me remove the necklace from her.

Thus, the smelliest band of ragamuffins came before the most powerful man in Emerald City to plead our cases.

"You have ten minutes—the clock starts now," said the obviously bored and irritated Right Reverend Emerald, the Divine. It was clear he had been told we'd rejected all his seductive ploys.

"My name is Dorothy Hope Gale," I said. "We've come to request a meeting with you because we were told you were the Wizard and could work magic in getting Dr. Chen a new heart, Pastor Leo some courage, my friend Maria a brain, and for me and Toe-Toe a place where we belong."

"What do you think I am—a wizard?" chuckled the Right Rev rather sardonically. "I can't do that. That takes a collection of very special powerful tokens—one of which is on your body, Miss Gale."

"Then why did you agree to see us?" I cried. "Why did you waste our time?"

"I only agreed to see you because my assistant, Tiffany, said you were wearing the shoes of the Wicked Witch of the East. Do you know how long I've been trying to get my hands on those shoes? I've been naming and claiming those shoes for years. Your butler tried to steal them off your feet when you fell asleep during the massage, but it appears they really are magical because no matter how hard he tried, the shoes wouldn't budge. I have a hunch that once the other token is collected along with those shoes, you all will get what you want, and I'll get what I want."

"What's the other token?" asked Dr. Chen.

"The golden golf club of the Purple Wicked Witch of the West," replied the Wizard. "She never goes anywhere without it—never lets it out of her hands. Apparently, she believes it's one of the sources of her power. I want it."

"Why don't you get it yourself?" asked Pastor Leo.

"She'd kill me, idiot—that's why," replied the Wizard.

"And she won't kill us?" I screeched.

"Not my problem, is it?" replied the Wizard. "Take it or leave it. If you want what you feel you need, then you need to get me that goddamned golf club. Dismissed!"

We asked around town and discovered the Purple Wicked Witch of the West was holding a rally on the outskirts of town that night. Dr. Chen thought we should get some items to help us blend in, so he and Maria procured some GMOMA hats, T-shirts, and rally flags.

The gatekeeper, Otto, then unlocked and removed the insufferable green sunglasses before we left the Emerald City. I vowed then and there to refuse to wear them again if we ever managed to complete our mission and return.

It didn't take us long to locate Purple's rally because the road was jammed with people flocking to the blazing floodlights that surrounded the stage. It was showtime! We pulled down our hats over our eyes as we wrestled our way to the front of the crowd.

The audience waiting for the Purple Wicked Witch of the West was a much smaller group of people than at the cathedral, but they were just as intense, although markedly angrier. It felt like if they knew of our intention to steal her talisman, they'd eat us alive. I wished we had something more formidable than purple ball caps, T-shirts, and flag poles. Pastor Leo had tried to bring in his rifle, but it was taken from him by the Wicked Witch of the West's armed guards at our entry point. But I need not have worried. As soon as the crowd ascertained that we were supporters by our purple regalia, they welcomed us into their fold with open arms.

At that moment, I had a modicum of sympathy for some of the

Purple's GMOMA supporters we met that night. They seemed to have gotten caught up in this madness in their search for a place to belong. As GMOMA supporters, they got to make friends, join a group with a common mission, be entertained by a clown, and at the end of the day, they went home feeling a little less lonely—a little less disconnected in a chaotic impersonal world. I could relate, somewhat.

A closer look revealed that the majority of the Purple's followers were die-hard groupies dripping with resentment against anyone who didn't support the Purple Wicked Witch of the West or their racist grievances. Many of them had been to a hundred rallies or more and they were more like rock concerts than political campaign rallies. In fact, most of them had slept there overnight to secure great standing areas to be close to the Purple when she arrived. They wore a variety of memorabilia, including purple hats, dresses, pants, sneakers, bookbags, and T-shirts that sported slogans in all caps, seemingly so as not to miss any opportunity to scream at *the others* if only from their chests:

"IF YOU DON'T LIKE THE PURPLE, THEN YOU PROBABLY WON'T LIKE ME, AND I'M OK WITH THAT!"
"I'M WITH THE PURPLE AND I MAKE NO APOLOGIES!"
"MA'ON IS MY GOD AND THE PURPLE WICKED WITCH OF THE WEST IS MY PRESIDENT!"

There were a couple of protestors who had snuck in, but they were quickly ferreted out, especially when one was caught wearing a T-shirt denigrating the Wicked Witch of the West:

"ONE THING I TRUST MORE THAN THE PURPLE:
Sharing a hot tub with a school of piranha

The Wicked Witch of the West ended up being hours late. But just as the crowd grew restless, music from the loudspeakers blasted what I immediately recognized as the chorus to *Purple Rain* by Prince.

The Purple was about six feet tall, and she was about as wide as she was tall, which caused her to slither across the stage as if she were roller skating from side to side in a concentrated slow-motion glide. Prince must have been rolling over in his grave. Her hair was crayon yellow and was teased into a bouffant that was one foot high. Purple's skin was a putrid pink color, and the texture was so stretched from her overindulgence in greasy, fatty foods, that the skin looked like pork rinds sewed together in a piecemeal fashion to form a face. The Purple Wicked Witch of the West was dressed all in purple and gold, and in her right hand, she carried a gold-plated golf club. When the Purple came to a full stop in front of the microphone at the podium, she raised the golf club in a salute to the crowd and they responded with outstretched right arms and palms down as they chanted: *"Heil Purple, Heil Purple, Heil Purple"* three times straight.

The four of us exchanged wide-eyed glances of horror, as I silently mouthed our one-line anthem that would encapsulate the experience of our first-time rally with the Purple: *"What the fuck?!"*

Chapter XIII

The Truth Shall Set Them Free

The Oz national anthem erupted from the loudspeakers and the heil purple hands snapped to allegiance. Hands were placed over hearts as a mellifluous male voice narrated a video featuring the Purple Wicked Witch of the West in various beatific poses. The audience started to weep, overcome by the glory they felt emanating from the Purple's presence as the words of the video flowed through their hearts, minds, and spirits:

> *"Ma'on looked down on his wonderland of Oz—his perfectly planned community, and he said, 'I need a caretaker,' so Ma'on gave us the Wicked Witch of the West..."*

I tuned out most of the video because I had to guard my heart from the seduction of idol worship as much as I needed to guard my spirit from the worship of greed at the House of Oz. Soon enough the idolatrous video concluded and the Purple began her surprisingly lethargic, monotonous speech.

"What a crowd. What a HUGE crowd. I'm seeing all my faithful here tonight," said the Purple.

"Where are my pious religious peeps?" asked the Purple. "I tell you; these people love me. You know why?" asked Purple Wicked Witch of the West as she looked into one of the TV cameras. "Cause I am sent from God to fulfill their agenda, so they tell me. I got them everything they wanted to consummate their *Ten Summit Plan* in Oz. I got them judges to do their bidding, destroyed women's rights, mangled civil rights—you name it, I butchered it. I can do anything and these pious folks will still support me because of all I've done for them.

"I could grab them by their genitalia, and they'd show up for me. I could even be accused of rape (not saying I'm admitting anything here), and you all would support me—wouldn't you? I could shoot someone on Munchkinville Avenue and you'd still have my back! Ain't that right, my pious ones?"

"THAT'S RIGHT, PURPLE!" yelled most of the crowd.

"And don't believe what the mainstream Oz media says about me," said the Purple. "It's a witch hunt! You just keep focusing on the truth, that I'm your precious savior, and once you get me back in office, I'll get my revenge. I'LL BE YOUR RETRIBUTION, TOO!"

"Now where are my Blacks? The Oz press keeps harping about how I'm a racist presidential candidate, but I love the Blacks. Where are you darkies? It's hard to see you under all these lights. Oh, there you are!" exclaimed the Wicked Witch of the West as she pointed to Pastor Leo and me.

"See, what did I tell you?" crowed the Purple. "Proof positive that the Blacks love me—cause they're here. I just want to let you two know that I'm standing in the breach for you as well as I am for my Whites. The vermin that are after you are after me too, and I'm taking the blows for you. Look no further, I am truly the anointed one you've been waiting for. I'm your Savior!

"Speaking of vermin—y'all may have heard that my campaign had a little trouble awhile back . . ."

"*BOOOOOOO!* replied the audience against the invisible vermin.

". . . Which was caused by some drag queen down in Munchkinville. My people told me that this spawn of vermin ran some kind of drag queen story hour as a side gig for the local libraries. But get this, his main job was as a community organizer to stir up trouble against your anointed one standing in the gap for you. Can you believe that?"

"BOO! BOO! BOOOO!" shouted the crowd. "Get rid of that she-man!"

"No worries," said the Wicked Witch of the West. "Already done. We shut down that pervert in a heartbeat. I'm not going to tell you how my people did it, but let's just say, the drag queen walks the Land of Oz no more. Remember when I told the Tiger-Bear boys—good people, I'll have you know—to stand down and stand by after a previous incident? Well . . . let's just say they're not standing down any longer.

"Ha! I just thought of something funny. Have you heard that old joke, 'If a drag queen screams when she's having her fancy painted fingernails pulled out by the roots, does she scream in a high-pitched voice or in the low-pitched voice God gave him when he was born?' *Hee, hee, hee, hee . . .*"

The cheering crowd drowned out my inadvertent screams of agony as I collapsed into Pastor Leo's arms. We probably would have been noticed and attacked at that point of the rally, but out of the midst of the crowd an otherworldly roar thundered through the horde—as if resounding from the rafters of heaven:

"ENOUGH!"

"KNEEL, PURPLE!"

"BEHOLD, YOUR GOD!"

The voice wasn't coming from the heavens though—it was coming from the middle of the crowd. As the throng made a wake for the person who was the bearer of the voice to come forward, a being about twelve feet tall, in a hooded robe, strode up to the stage, and towered over the Wicked Witch of the West. He threw back his hood and the most extraterrestrial, benevolent, glorious face turned to scan the audience and rested on our family of four for what seemed like an eternity, but it was only a few seconds. Then the figure turned back to gaze at the Wicked Witch of the West and his facial expression turned into a furious storm that was too fearsome to look upon.

"SAY MY NAME, PURPLE!" commanded the being.

"I have no idea who you are. Security! SECURITY! Get this illegal alien out of my rally," whined the Purple.

"Oh, really?" replied the being. "You've been doing a very bad impersonation of me for years. Surely you know the name of the god whose glory you've been stealing."

The audience saw a stream of yellow liquid seep out from underneath the purple gown of the Wicked Witch of the West—almost as if she were melting—as she recoiled and shriveled in fear before the being.

"I don't know you," whined Purple. "Look what you made me do —I peed myself! Go away! Don't kill me!"

"Of course, you don't recognize me. It's because you *never* knew me," said the being. "I AM MA'ON!"

We all fell to our knees and the Purple crumbled even further.

"I don't plan to kill you, Purple. If I were going to do that, I would have done so ages ago. You are the worst of the worst. In fact, death is much too good for you. What *I am* going to do to you is so much worse. I'm going to strip you of your power over people and wake them from their long nightmarish coma of your lies. I'm going to allow people to see you as you really are—a sniveling, pathetic, cowardly, ignorant, lying, snake of a person.

"What I bequeath you with, Purple, is a long life of ignobility, ignominy, disdain, and mockery. As soon as I wave my hand over this crowd, you will be forgotten, ignored, and disgraced. You will lose your popularity and your voice—never to be seen or heard from again. In an instant, your followers will know that you've been lying to them all along."

On that note, Ma'on turned to the crowd, and slowly waved his hand over us. The people stumbled around as if waking from a dream. Some of them started crying in bitter disappointment, some screamed in agony, and others fled the scene. Many of them knelt in homage to God —the real one. If they didn't, they were smacked down into a face-plant by some invisible force. Just about everyone turned their backs against the abomination on the stage as it sobbed uncontrollably in its urine-soaked purple robe.

Ma'on left the stage and walked straight toward our family. We all bowed in honor of his presence, and as he lifted each one of our heads so that he could gaze into our eyes, he blessed us with his love.

"Maria," said Ma'on. "Thank you for the service you've performed for your friends. You are *so smart*. It's time you let go of your husband's false description of your mind. He lied. You have the brains I gave you and those brains brought your newfound family to this point in their journey. Believe me when I tell you, your brain will guide them to the conclusion of their stories. Trust yourself.

"Pastor Leo, you are a man after my own heart—full of passion, and a heart for the vulnerable. You have a genuine desire to see goodness and love permeate Oz. Although a bit impetuous, you have undying compassion for your fellow man. Your courage has kept you and your friends safe from false doctrine. You've always been a courageous man—you just need to follow through to the finale of the hard road set before you.

"Dr. Chen—my 'Tin' man—your Daiyu sends you her love, and says to tell you that she'll see you soon. She told me to tell you that your heart has not gone missing nor is it beyond repair. You just need to expand it to include others along with your memory of her. The heart knows no boundaries of love. It looks to me as if you have already started her assignment with the collection of this new family of yours.

"Dorothy Hope Gale, it is a pleasure to meet you. I have loved you all of your life. I want you to know that *I see you*. All good things that came to you in life came from me, including your friendship with Jonathan. You won't be able to recognize it tonight, but soon—*very soon*—you'll find where you belong and then you'll go home.

"Oh, by the way, Dottie, I think this belongs to you," Ma'on said as he handed me the Wicked Witch of the West's golden golf club.

"Now I've got to go. So many people to see, so much evil to defeat."

Just like that, Ma'on disappeared as quickly as he had appeared, and we four friends knew—beyond the shadow of a doubt—we'd never be the same again.

Chapter XIV

Somebody's Ass is Gonna be Grass

"OPEN THIS GODDAMN DOOR, OTTO!" I screamed as Pastor Leo incessantly pulled the cord to the gate doorbell while the rest of us furiously pounded the door as the dawn of a new day began to crest over the Emerald City.

Returning to the city from the Purple rally had been extremely slow going because a couple thousand people had stumbled along the highways and byways in a stupor—shell-shocked from their encounter with real power, real glory, real majesty, real truth. The Wicked Witch of the West's rally attendees didn't seem to care where they were going, they just wanted to get as far away as possible from Purple's screams of agony which thundered through the air for miles and miles as the rally escapees covered their ears to drown out the heartbreaking sound.

Purple's agony of being robbed of attention, adoration, and worship elicited such a deep, wretched cry of abandonment that I've often thought many times since that incident it must be what going to Hell is like: a vulnerable baby, left alone in the dark, crying for his mother— over and over again—but she never comes—no one *ever answers* the lonely call of the abandoned child left in a realm of pitch-black darkness. An eternity of no love, no embraces, no laughter, no joy, no hope.

"HEY!" screamed Otto the gatekeeper from the open portal at the top of the wall. "What is wrong with you fools? The entire city is asleep except for the bakers and the candlestick makers."

"Get your ass down here NOW and let us in," demanded Maria. "We have a bone to pick with your boss."

Otto must have sensed the urgency in our pleas because the little man scampered down the back ladder of the door and opened it with the alacrity of a Bulgarian wedding greeter.

"Well, hello, my friends," said Otto as he bowed in deep honor to the gang of four. "Welcome back! I was just putting on a show up there because the Wizard tapes all my up-top greetings. But I truly am over-joyed to see you all. How is it that you're still alive? I never expected to see you again on this side of the veil."

"Does the Wizard do that often?" asked Dr. Chen. "Send people who annoy him to a Purple rally knowing the Wicked Witch of the West will do his dirty work and get rid of them?"

"Pretty much," said a chagrined Otto. "No one has ever returned—you're the first."

"Well, it must be a sign," said Pastor Leo. "Otto, we need to see the Wizard now!"

"He's still in bed, and I was warned not to disturb him tonight upon pain of death," replied Otto.

"Otto, you seem like a good man," I said. "It's imperative we see the Wizard at this very moment—unannounced. If you are truly overjoyed to see us then I need you to trust us."

Otto nodded his head in resigned agreement and pulled out a box of green sunglasses to lock over our eyes.

"No thanks, buddy," said Dr. Chen, as he pushed the box of glasses aside. "I have a feeling these glasses are a subterfuge to keep us from seeing things as they really are in the Emerald City. Hey, it's almost dawn. What time does the changing of the guard happen?"

"Probably not going to happen today," replied Otto. "The Wizard sent most of the guards to the Purple rally to keep an eye on you all, but they have not returned. I have no idea why. The few that were left went out on the town and tied one on—courtesy of the Wizard. It would take an earthquake to wake them before noon. However, the security cameras are in full operation, and there are tripwires throughout the cathedral and all around RRED's suite."

"What can you do to help us with that, Otto, my friend?" pleaded Maria.

It didn't take Otto more than a heartbeat to volunteer that he could shut off the alarms and all the tripwires throughout the cathedral to let us proceed without interference.

"Just give me a five-minute head start," Otto said as he opened the inner door to the city, and began closing down switches in the electrical box just inside the city gate.

"Otto, why are you really helping us?" queried Pastor Leo.

"Tiffany is my daughter," whispered a trembling Otto, as he scurried up the hill toward the Emerald Cathedral.

The door to the Wizard's suite was unlocked. He clearly did not expect anyone to disturb him that night as he had been careless with securing his inner sanctum.

As the four of us quietly opened the door to the living room and crept toward his bedroom, I could hear a woman crying and moaning in pain on the other side of the door. On the silent count of three, Pastor Leo, with his rifle in hand; Dr. Chen with his cane held high; me, with Purple's gold golf club; and Maria, wielding a steak knife she'd picked up off the room-service cart as we passed it; slowly turned the door knobs of the double doors and charged into the bedroom just as the naked Wizard raised his arm and brought down the buckle end of his belt against Tiffany's naked body as she screamed in pain.

Before RRED could attempt another strike, Pastor Leo and Dr. Chen grabbed the Wizard and wrestled him to the ground—threatening to blow his brains out if he moved. Maria and I ran to Tiffany who had crawled into a fetal position, and we covered her in a sheet and our embraces.

"Tiffany, baby girl—look at me," I demanded. Her bloodshot eyes rolled around in her head for a brief moment as her blood-soaked green hair fell over her face. At first, she didn't respond, but then she zoned in on my face, forced a weak smile, and whispered, "Hi Dottie," before she faded away again.

"I think he drugged her," said Maria. "She can't seem to focus for very long."

"Yeah, that, and it looks as if he's practically beat her to death," I said. "Tiffany Baby—please focus. Can you hear me? Are you OK? Can you stand up? Where are your clothes, honey?"

Tiffany slowly pointed to the lounge chair across the room with a shaky arm. She was covered in bruises from head to toe, but Maria and I determined that she could still walk if one of us supported her.

"Maria, help her get dressed and take her to her father," I commanded. "Help him get her the medical attention she needs, and then have him send any police he can trust. I'll stay here and help the guys restrain the Wizard. *Hurry!*"

I heard Pastor Leo cock the rifle as he pointed it against the Wizard's forehead, and said, "If you even move an inch, I will blow your mother-fuckin' face off. I'm so angry right now that it won't take much from you to cause me to lose my religion on your ass. Do I make myself clear?"

The fear in the Right Rev's eyes was palpable. Judging by the mound of cocaine on the coffee table and the empty bottles of alcohol on the floor, RRED was almost on the verge of collapsing. We tore up one of the Wizard's silk sheets into strips, tied them together, and bound him to one of the bedroom chairs. Dr. Chen made some very strong coffee, and over the next hour or so, we were able to get RRED sober enough to answer our questions.

"Aren't you married, pervert?" asked Pastor Leo, never letting his rifle move from the target of the Wizard's forehead.

"Wife's leading a women's retreat in the mountains," sputtered the Wizard.

"So, this is how you play, when the wife is away—raping and tormenting young women?" I asked with scorn.

"I . . . um . . . we . . . have an understanding . . .." stammered RRED.

"The question was rhetorical, asshole," I said. "It's pretty clear you're a monster."

For the first time that night, the Wizard noticed that I was in possession of the gold golf club. "I don't suppose you'll give me that talisman? If you do, I'll let you go back to wherever you came from, and we'll call it even-Steven—the Wicked Witch of the West's golden golf club in exchange for your freedom and your life."

"God, check out the hubris on this dude," I said. "You're tied up, we have the gun and a knife, and any moment now the police and the Hound of Heaven are going to come looking for your ass and you are going to wish we had killed you."

"The Hound of who . . .?" asked the Wizard.

"You'll find out soon enough," I said. "Let's just say, it's a horrible thing to be a rapist and end up in the hands of an angry god."

"You were never going to give us what we came here for, were you?" asked Maria as she entered the room followed by Otto and four burly policemen.

"Bitch, you all were going to *give me* what I wanted," snarled the Wizard. "All I needed to consolidate my power and control over Oz was the magic of the three witches: the shoes from the Wicked Witch of the East, the golden golf club from the Wicked Witch of the West, and the kiss mark on Dottie's forehead from the Wicked Witch of the North."

"Kiss mark?" I said, trying to figure out what in the world the Wizard was talking about as I checked out my reflection in the mirror on the wall beside me.

"The mark that the Witch of the North must have placed on your forehead," growled RRED. "I noticed it immediately from the pulpit when I first saw you in the sanctuary during the church service. It's the power that has protected you and your simpleton friends from harm.

That's why I figured you'd have a halfway chance of getting close to Purple and grabbing the golf club because of the protective force of the kiss. I've sent many others, but Purple turned them into toast before they could even say their names. If you thought I could help you get home or wherever you belonged, then I could be assured you'd return with what I wanted.

"Of course, I wasn't going to give you any such thing, even if I could, which I can't. I planned to lock you and your friends in our cathedral catacombs until you died, but by that time, Oz would be completely under our Crusader control from the womb to the government and Purple would have served her purpose and been cast to the side or had a heart attack from her gluttonous diet. Our Oz Crusaderism-Nationalist group has been using her just like she thinks she's using us. We let her think she was the embodiment of some ancient queen sent to us by Ma'on to save Oz from its 'sins' while we consolidated our power over all of Oz."

"Nope, he wasn't going to give you one goddamned thing, that's for sure," replied an apoplectic Otto as he tackled the Wizard and repeatedly punched him in the face until he broke the Wizard's jaw.

"All he does is take, and take, and gives little in return," seethed a hysterical Otto. "I've watched him do this for years—take advantage of vulnerable people—but turned my back on his destructive behavior because I felt he represented Ma'on, and who among us is perfect? But this time, he came for my family, *my daughter* . . .," said a choked-up Otto who collapsed in a sobbing, exhausted heap.

When Otto finally pulled himself together, he introduced us to his four police officer friends whom he said he trusted implicitly. Two of them were Tiffany's uncles and the other two were Otto's best friends since childhood. At the orders of Otto, the police officers took RRED to the inner bowels of the prison—the dungeon. Judging by the engorged fury on their faces, I often wondered if the Wizard ever made it into the jail in one piece. I'm told he never made it out of that dungeon—that's for sure.

"Now what do we do?" I asked as the exhaustion from the previous day suddenly turned my body into a wet noodle and dragged me to the floor.

"We came here to get answers for our lives from a man who was a sham. After all our struggles and a near-death experience, I'm no closer to belonging anywhere than I was before. At least Ma'on gave you guys some clarity. What do Toe-Toe and I do now?"

Tears streamed down my face as the weariness and the despair upended every ounce of my last bit of courage. Otto hugged me with all his might and did what only a good father can do—take care of us by first imposing the practical: "Let's get out of this temple of horror. I suggest you come with me and let me book you into the best B&B in Oz —my home. You all need to get a good night's sleep, and then we'll set up a solid strategy for the rest of Dottie's quest. I just need to pull together all the particulars. Will you trust me?"

"Sure, why not," I said, not having the energy to contest his suggestions.

"Excellent! Tomorrow, after much-needed sleep, you are off to meet Glinda—The Good Witch of the South," said Otto. "She'll know what to do and how to do it. Glinda is the most powerful of all the witches and her castle stands on the edge of the desert. Glinda is a true friend of Ma'on's, and in the end, you'll grow to realize that coming to the Emerald City was indeed part of your destiny, and Otto the gate-keeper was your North Star to Glinda, the Good Witch of the South."

CHAPTER XV

A Lion is Offered a Kingdom

The smells of bacon cooking, coffee percolating, waffles baking, and fried onions, green peppers, and mushrooms simmering to join in sisterhood with a fluffy cheese omelet were the smells that brought me back to Oz from a nightmare that was threatening to consume me.

My eyes opened to a luscious pink-on-pink room of a teenager who had long ago moved out, but whose parents couldn't bear parting with the altar of trophies attributed to their darling girl's specialness. There was Tiffany as head cheerleader, Tiffany on the swim team, Tiffany in the school play, Tiffany at her senior prom, and the beaming Tiffany graduating from college—the world as her oyster. The evil of the world —especially via the betrayal of her faith—had not surged up on the shores of Tiffany's life yet, and my heart broke as I wondered if that innocent little girl would be lost to her parents forever.

On the armchair across the room, there was a complete safari outfit, replete with an adorable safari hat with a note pinned to the top indicating that they were for me and that I should join everyone for breakfast when I felt up to it.

After I took a shower and got dressed, I started to descend the stairs into the kitchen when raucous waves of laughter rose from the crowd of people seated around an extremely large kitchen table that was laden with enough food to feed an army.

"Dorothy," said Otto as he sprang from his chair and greeted me with a waist-high bear hug when I walked into the room, "Welcome to our home."

"I'd like you to meet my lovely wife, Astrid," said Otto as he beamed with overflowing affection toward her. Astrid was twice Otto's size and had long ago lost her girlish figure, but he didn't seem to notice. The love that flowed from their eyes to each other was extremely poignant.

Astrid rushed to me and enveloped me in her arms and refused to let me go for the longest time as she whispered, "Thank you, thank you, thank you . . . may Ma'on bless you!" Then she took me around and introduced me to everyone seated at the breakfast table—never letting go of my hand: Three girls and one boy, all tall towheaded Scandinavian young adults in their 20s and 30s—Tiffany was clearly the baby of the family. Their father was the only short, squat Munchkin of swarthy complexion among them. I could see the delighted expression on Dr. Chen's face out of the corner of my eye as he pondered the conundrum of this genetic cocktail.

Two towheaded toddler grandchildren sat in high chairs and lobbed hashbrown potatoes at anyone within their reach and surreptitiously slipped sausages to Toe-Toe who seemed to be having a ball as she ran in and out from underneath the table jumping up to grab the toddlers' goodies. Anyone looking at that prosaic tableau would never have guessed that less than thirty-six hours ago my friends and I had danced with the devil and his henchman and won.

After basking in the warmth and beautiful love of Otto's family, I forced myself to break the spell and ask about the welfare of Tiffany and our next plan of action.

"The doctor said that she'll fully recover, but it's going to take a long time," Astrid said, wiping tears from her eyes with the lower part of her apron. "Dr. Russell said we should bring her home after she's released—that he could heal her body, but only the love of family could heal her soul. I have to believe that or I will go crazy."

"Believe it, dear," said Otto, as he patted his wife's hand. "Our family love is expansive enough to assuage the worst terror. Our Tiff's going to make it—you wait and see!"

We all sat in uncomfortable silence for a bit, hoping beyond hope that the faith Otto had in their family love would be enough to bring Tiffany back from the brink. In the meantime, I sensed it was time to move on down the road.

"Thank you, Astrid and Otto, for the wonderful hospitality you've provided us and for the safari clothes," I said. "Where did you get these and how did you know our sizes?"

"I own an All-Things Safari Adventure store," said Otto's daughter, "and Dad supplied me with your sizes. He's got a pretty good eye if I do say so myself."

"That I do," chuckled Otto. "My son here picked up a souped-up RAV-4 for your travels to the Good Witch of the South's domain. We strapped on a ladder to the top because if my memory serves me correctly, you're going to need one to scale the barrier of the Sect of the Walled Off or the Chosen Ones if they are locked down for any reason, which is most of the time."

We reluctantly gathered our things and headed toward the RAV4 golf cart in the driveway, when Otto pulled Pastor Leo aside. "Pastor Leo, the Emerald Cathedral could use a new pastor—a real man of Ma'on. Won't you stay and lead us? It has to be someone with great courage to rebuild what the cankerworm of the Wizard has destroyed."

"Oh," said Pastor Leo, clearly humbled. "I'll think about it, I promise I will, but first I must get Dottie safely through the unknown territories to Glinda's estate. Once I've done that, I'll return and we can discuss the pros and cons of such a magnanimous offer."

"That's a deal," said Otto. "Dr. Chen, I have a feeling that once we uncover all the harm that the Wizard has done to his congregation, we're all going to need some serious therapy. Would you and Maria consider resettling in Emerald City to create a center of healing?"

Dr. Chen and Maria looked at each other and smiled a bit as they nodded their acquiescence to Otto's invitation. "It would be our pleasure," said a very invigorated Dr. Chen as Maria clapped in delight.

While we stood alongside our vehicle, Astrid and her son waddled out of the house carrying a huge box between them which was overladen with food and four overstuffed backpacks with even more food, camping supplies, and first aid kits. We all laughed as Otto noted that Astrid had packed enough food to feed all of Emerald City.

"You must call us as soon as you arrive safely at the Good Witch of the South's castle, dears," said Astrid. "Otto and I will be worried sick about you."

"Now Astrid," said Otto, "they're not children. They've come this far. They've outed the Wizard, toppled Purple, and rescued our Tiffany. I think they will be just fine."

We all kissed and hugged and kissed and hugged again, assuring each other that it would not be the last time we'd spend in each other's company because we had all become extended family. Finally, we drove away from Otto and Astrid's lovely home, waving until they weren't visible anymore, and headed into the horizon of the final leg of my adventure to find where I belonged.

It was hard to explain, but I could sense Toe-Toe and I were almost done—almost at the end—and I could hardly wait.

Chapter XVI

Until We Meet Again

Before we got in the golf cart, Otto had slipped me a letter and asked me to read it to everyone once we were back on the road. Pastor Leo drove, I sat shotgun, and Dr. Chen and Maria sat behind us. Maria had been softly crying as we pulled away from the lovely gatekeeper's family, and Dr. Chen gently held her in his arms, bringing what comfort he could to a woman mourning a marriage and a family she always hoped for but never had.

"Do you mind if I read Otto's letter to us at this point?" I asked as I put on my reading glasses. "It probably has a lot of prescient information for the journey up ahead."

My Beautiful Friends—my courageous angels: My family and I have no proper words with which to thank you for the way you saved our precious Tiffany's life. For as long as we live, we will owe you a great debt of gratitude, and you will always be welcome in our home.

I must confess, Astrid and I are mortified at how we fell asleep at the wheel while traveling under the passport of a false doctrine. We allowed ourselves to follow a candidate whose life as a liar, an abuser, a hater, a cheater, and a grand manipulator numbed us to the truth of who she really was. And when the Wizard fell under her spell and declared

Purple the anointed one, we fell right into line without questioning any of it. Because of our blindness, we almost paid the ultimate price.

It is good that you are making your way to the Good *Witch of the South's territory. While you were sleeping, we received a lot of phone calls —some good—many disturbing. We lost so many friends to the idolatry of the Purple Wicked Witch of the West. The Emerald Cathedral worshiped her as the second coming of Ma'on. Since Purple was exposed and humiliated at the rally, people are waking up from her chokehold on their minds —some are grateful and horrified at the conspiracy theories they swallowed hook, line, and sinker. But most of my friends and neighbors refused to admit they were wrong; they won't let go of the lies because to do so would mean that they had been wrong about everything all along, and that would mean they'd have to walk a road of humility that their pride won't permit. The friends of Purple will come looking for you, and the sooner you get under Glinda's protection, the better. I suggest you take the straightest route to her kingdom which will mean cutting through the land of the Walled Off and that of the Auntie Trolls for Liberty. To go around their lands would eat up too much time.*

No one has figured out where the Wizard is yet. They all surmise he went into hiding once the Wicked Witch of the West was exposed. I plan to keep that illusion going for as long as possible to buy you some time.

Purple's strongest control was in the South. I believe you'll have to make your way through several hostile territories. The first barrier to breach will be the Gnarly Fighting Trees which is a stronghold for the government officials who have pledged their allegiance to Purple. I have no insight as to how to overcome them—but I hear they have all fled to the area of the Gnarly Fighting Trees to try and salvage their ruling power. Once you locate the grove of trees, you'll need to infiltrate their camp. My daughter packed some GMOMA paraphernalia you can use and put on to help you blend in.

As I mentioned before, the second and third strongholds, before you reach the border of the Good *Witch of the South's estate, are The Walled Off, better known as The Frozen Chosen, and the Auntie Trolls for Liberty fortresses. The Frozen Chosen have nothing to do with the Purple or the*

Wizard—that's because they have nothing to do with anyone outside of themselves.

They live in isolation from the rest of the world because they believe being stuck in a time warp of a hundred years ago is the best way to honor God, and they really don't care what happens to the so-called heathens beyond their borders. Their religious theory is that they are the only ones going to Heaven so they are just biding time until the rest of us are destroyed and Ma'on returns to take them to his kingdom in the sky. Don't expect any help from them, unless it is to get you off their property as quickly as possible. Just tiptoe through their land as politely and as quickly as you can to get to the Good Witch of the South's territory.

The Auntie Trolls for Liberty took it upon themselves to control what we all read and confiscated or burned any books they thought were offensive according to their standards of "righteousness." They were the proponents of the movement to shame trans and queer citizens of Oz by making it against the law to speak the truth about who they were. It will take a long time to bring the Auntie Trolls for Liberty back into a connected, cooperative, caring society. The self-righteous are always the hardest nuts to crack.

When you reach the Frozen Chosen area, you might need the ladder on the roof of the RAV4 golf cart to get over the wall that surrounds their hideout. They will be so shocked that you've invaded their sanctified space that they won't give you much pushback—especially once they know you're just passing through—I hope.

*The Auntie Trolls are another thing. They are like any trolls you've read about. You can't get through their territory without guessing riddles that they think they are the only ones who know the answer to, since these particular trolls burned all the riddle books in the last book-banning event they organized with the blessing of the Wizard. The good news is that my daughter squirreled away a major tome of riddles—***The Great Riddle Book of Oz***—at the beginning of the burnings and kept it hidden in the basement. She has included it underneath the sandwiches. Memorize it! You're going to need it.*

Until we meet again—Ma'on speed, my friends.

CHAPTER XVII

The Gnarly Politicians

We found the overgrown grove without any trouble because the chaotic fighting that could be heard a half mile down the road led us right to it. It seemed as if most of the two hundred or so right-wing politicians from the Oz Congress were in attendance yelling and screaming at each other. We found a way to slip in under the mammoth trees while still in our golf cart and quietly drove to the back of the conference and parked underneath a thicket of a very dense stand of tall shrubs.

There were megaphones sporadically placed throughout the crowd, and the stage was well amplified, so it wasn't difficult to hear anyone in the crowd, although it was hard to see the faces on stage. Pastor Leo found a pair of binoculars in the glove compartment, and at Maria's insistence, gave them to her because she said she knew all the players who were speaking.

"See that woman on the left—the bleached blond whose hair is the texture of straw and whose voice is so strident and face is so apoplectic that she looks as if she's going to spontaneously combust?" asked Maria. "That's MTG, Mary Thomas Gray. She's the one who claims to sit at the right hand of Purple *and* also claims Ma'on is her main man—so to speak. She wears a huge symbol of Ma'on around her neck so that no one forgets what a 'good believer' she is. She's so pious her shit doesn't smell. Her manipulation and cruelty are legendary."

"Who is the little man she's pounding into the floor with a gavel," I asked.

"That's MJ—formally known as Matt Jackson," said Maria. "He's been Speaker of the House of Oz for a hot minute. Looks like he's on his way out if MTG has anything to do with it. Apparently, he played too nicely in the sandbox with the opposition for MTG's liking. However, I recently heard that he redid his pledge of allegiance to the Purple just before Ma'on appeared in Oz, so he might be safe from MTG's wrath for a while, but as to the wrath of Ma'on . . . ."

"Who is the sniveling guy with the bad comb-over, the dithering walk, and the puckered lips on the other side of MTG?" I asked.

"He's LG, Lester Groan," replied Maria. "See how he's bent over almost into a horseshoe shape? That's because he has no spine. It disintegrated years ago when the Purple Wicked Witch of the West first came into power. LG's body got calcified into that shape when he permanently affixed his lips to Purple's ass, and they got stuck to Purple's posterior like the magic shoes on your feet," laughed Maria.

"Seriously, Maria," I chuckled. "You should be ashamed of yourself."

"Well, it's almost true—he's such a sycophant," said Maria. "All three of them are a piece of work! But MTG is the worst. She wallows in outlandish conspiracy theories, pushes tons of anti-Semitic tropes, and accuses people from the opposite party of being elite child-sacrificing devil worshipers!"

"Lord have mercy," I said. "Who is that bald Black guy running toward the stage screaming, 'I LOVE MY PURPLE! I LOVE HER—I SURE DO! Where is my Purple? Lord have mercy, is it true, she's gone? Is it true I've lost my one true love?'"

"That disgusting piece of crap is TS—better known as Tom Spot," said Pastor Leo. "His obsequiousness knows no bounds. Those are just a few of the people who propped up the Purple Wicked Witch of the

West in the name of their *Ten Summit Crusader* cause. I shudder to think what would have happened to Oz had they completed what they considered their God-given mission."

"The thing that stands out about most of the Ozians who supposedly are disciples of Ma'on is their cruelty," I said. "*They are so goddamn mean! I* thought Ma'on was a god of love. His followers sure don't represent him well. Why would anyone want to get on board with a god whose followers treat you like a piece of shit unless you agree with them? Is this the best they can do? From the Wicked Witch of the East to the Wizard to these politicians, they all make me want to bring out the booze and just keep dancing!"

"Exactly," said a very sad Pastor Leo. "I've been praying for years that Ma'on would rise up against this antithetical assault against his character because good-hearted people are fleeing his churches in droves. But it's as if the heavens were brass until recently. . .."

Suddenly, without warning, a booming voice the four of us immediately recognized erupted from the back of the crowd: **"ENOUGH! ENOUGH! E-N-O-U-G-H!"**

The crowd stopped in their tracks as Ma'on strode to the stage and grabbed the gavel from MTG's hands.

"Who the fu . . .." MTG started to say to the stranger until he turned his angry gaze on her which made her drop to her knees.

"Oh my God," gasped MTG.

"You've got that right," said Ma'on to everyone in the audience. "And I've come to stop your madness. I am Ma'on, the God you claim to love and serve. But I don't know you—none of you—nothing about you is created in my image."

"Well, these fools may not know you, but I sure do, my Lord," said MTG, as she bowed in a clumsy obsequious manner.

"Not everyone who calls me Lord is of my kingdom," said Ma'on.

"But my Lord, didn't I prophesy in your name just last week?" said MTG. "I prophesied that the earthquake and the eclipse that happened near the people I don't like was a sign from you that you wanted Oz to repent or else you'd bring down hellfire and damnation all over Oz except where me and mine live, of course! And . . . and what about these demons I'm about to cast out of the Speaker of the House of Oz when I kick his ass to the curb because he didn't do what I told him to do? They just haven't learned yet that you, Ma'on, made me queen of this trash heap and I'm fulfilling my calling. Plus, I've also got a couple of miracles up my sleeve if you just hold on a bit. All of this I'm doing in *your name,* by the way—the name of Ma'on! How do you like those apples? I'm your right-hand woman, and I get the job done!"

Ma'on didn't say a word. He just stared at MTG until her overly bleached head burst into flames and the holy emblem on her chest exploded. Then he broke off a large tree branch from the gigantic tree overhanging the stage and started knocking the Purple minions here, there, and everywhere—recalling a memory in my mind of an incarnate being from another time, in another place, who cleansed a temple by thrashing the moneychangers and the greedy merchants out of a temple as he accused them of being an abomination and a den of thieves.

"As much fun as this is to watch, I think it's time we get a move on before we get fricasseed," whispered Dr. Chen.

Memory is an odd and unreliable thing, but sometimes it can be a stand-up comedian when it returns to an amnesiac's brain—especially in a tense situation. As we gingerly and quietly tried to extract ourselves from Ma'on starring in his God of Wrath role against a few hundred gnarly politicians in the Gnarly Forest, I suddenly remembered the opening of a James Weldon Johnson poem: *Young man, young man, your arm's too short to box with God,* and it cracked me up!

I started to giggle uncontrollably, which infected Maria and Dr. Chen, whose laughter careened into Pastor Leo as he tried to maneuver the cart to the exit. It didn't take long for him to explode and join us in rounds of boisterous laughter that caused us all to simultaneously pee our pants.

"Stop, stop, stop," said Maria as she giggled even louder. "Someone will hear us."

"Well, Maria," I said between hiccups of laughter, "I really wish you had procured some of those old-people pee pads for our journey, because at least three old people just lost their dignity."

No one in the crowd paid attention to our laughter as we exited stage left and rolled on down the highway toward Glinda Land. They were all too occupied with trying to hide from a God who'd just announced it was repentance time for MTG and her crew, and that the piper had come to get paid.

CHAPTER XVIII

The Frozen Chosen

After the hysterical laughter wore off and got replaced with contemplative exhaustion, not one of us spoke as we traveled to the Frozen Chosen community. We had no words to describe what we had seen in the Gnarly Forest. On one hand, it was exhilarating and momentarily hilarious to see Ma'on right the wrongs of the misguided crusaders and save Oz. But on the other hand, one couldn't help but feel sorry for the gnarly politicians because falling into the hands of an angry God that one had blasphemed in the lust for power was nothing any human being could survive.

Before we knew it, we came upon a highway sign that said:

TURN LEFT FOR THE FROZEN CHOSEN COMPOUND;
TOURIST CURIO SHOPS CLOSED FOR MAINTENANCE;
SEE YOU NEXT YEAR.

"Well, that's a fine how-do-you-do," said Dr. Chen. "How are we supposed to cross through their land if they are closed for business?"

"We'll just have to find a way," I said. "Didn't Otto say that is why he had supplied us with a ladder because we might need it to scale the barrier of the Walled Off? We have no choice but to proceed even if we will be trespassing."

Taking the left turn brought us to the wall of the community in about twenty minutes. As we rounded the bend off the highway onto a private drive, the most magnificent wall of colorful blown glass rose up before us. Unlike the Emerald City, there seemed to be no door in which we could drive through nor a bell to ring to summon a gatekeeper to our aid.

Pastor Leo and Dr. Chen untied the ladder and gingerly placed it against the beautiful blown glass wall. Carrying our backpacks, we climbed the ladder one by one. When we reached the top and sat down on the wall, we gasped at the amazing beauty of what appeared before us, which caused us to say in unison: *"Oh, my God, this is glorious!"*

The land before us was quite expansive and dotted with large-scale glass blown houses, churches with steeples, parks, animals, and people going back and forth. There were roads but the only mode of transportation seemed to be an old-fashioned trolley car on tracks. There was not a golf cart in sight. Although everything was made of glass, if the wall was any indication of its sturdiness, we wouldn't have much to worry about.

We pulled the ladder up and over to the other side of the wall, threw down our backpacks to the dirt below us, and ascended one by one onto the shoulder of the roadway below as we set off to make our way across town to the other side—keeping due south.

A profusion of colors soon titillated our senses as we gazed in wonderment at the spiraling tall sunbursts suspended in the air, the large multicolored glass balls that floated in colorful glass boats down a rainbow-colored stream, and the fuchsia, orange, and aquamarine trees that swayed in a slight breeze causing the thin branches to clink against each other and make the musical sounds of Japanese wind chimes.

As we walked through the town, we passed a smattering of vibrant glass houses with even more brilliant flower gardens surrounding them. At one point, a pink and purple glass squirrel dashed across our path, and Toe-Toe sprang from my arms to chase him. Doing so caused the squirrel to crash into a man who then crashed into a horse he was leading by the reins, breaking one of the horse's legs.

"Oops," I said. "Looks like we were wrong about the delicacy of this land of glass."

"Look what you made me do!" yelled a navy-blue-and-cream glass man at Toe-Toe. "Contain your monster, you wicked woman, or I shall have you thrashed! Now I'm going to have to take him to the glass factory and have his leg glued back on. What do you mean by trespassing on our land and scaring the sand out of us?"

"Oh! I'm so sorry," I said as I captured Toe-Toe. "I didn't mean to cause you harm and neither did my dog."

The navy-blue-and-cream man made of glass simply huffed in irritation at me and scurried down the road leading his horse who was hobbling on three legs behind him.

"Thrashed?" I queried. "Where did we just set foot? In the 1930s?"

"More like the 1800s," responded Maria. "My dad told me about these people. They are immigrants and they are followers of Ma'on, but they feel their holiness is best expressed in freezing their lives in the time before science and technology advanced humankind in any significant way. They don't drive automated vehicles, have TVs, use cell phones, or mingle with the unorthodox—which would be the lot of us.

"The Frozen Chosen didn't start out as blown glass, but the longer they stayed locked away from the rest of the world, the more they became calcified, so to speak. According to my dad, my great-grandpa invited them to be a part of the original settlement and to even sit on the board to help plan the vision for Oz, but they refused because they thought it would be a sin. He gave them a wide berth and left them alone out of respect for their beliefs. They don't vote, they don't intermingle in our politics, and they don't rub elbows with us except to sell their wares at the curio shops throughout Oz. They don't even have electricity. They shun all of modernity. I suppose there is something a little charming about their way of life."

"Well, I for one, don't find them charming—I find them problematic," said Pastor Leo. "I've had the privilege and the misfortune of counseling some of their members who escaped from here. Living here isn't as idyllic as it seems. Like all groups of people, there is a lot of over-looked pain running beneath the beauty of their glass blown shells. Ma'on made humans in a way that they would need one another—support one another—no matter where we came from or what our beliefs are. How's this group any different than what the GMOMA people were trying to do? Here in blown glass land, it's either their way or the highway. No individualism, no women's rights, no independent thought allowed. Personally, I'd rather live in the mess that is our world than in a sheltered glass house that sees only its own reflection."

"Oh-oh, look," I said. "Someone has blown the whistle. There is quite a committee headed our way."

"Good afternoon," said the rainbow-colored glass man who led the group of concerned citizens. "I am Mayor Rainbow, and these are members of our city council. Why are you here and what do you want?"

"I'm sure you've heard of the demise of the Purple Wicked Witch of the West and her henchman, the Wizard?" said Dr. Chen.

"Nope!" responded Mayor Rainbow. "Neither do we care. What you heathens do in the dark needs to stay in the dark."

"See, this is what I'm talking about," whispered Pastor Leo to me. Turning back toward the mayor, he said, "How long do you think your precious, isolated glass world would have been allowed to function undisturbed had Purple gotten re-elected? It would have simply been a matter of short time before your place was raided, your land stolen, and you and your people scattered to places unknown, if you were lucky, because you were considered illegal immigrants in her book. Man, sticking your head in the sand is not the way to survive our crazy world. Becoming involved in it is the only way."

"How dare you trespass on my land and insult me?" said Mayor Rainbow.

Jumping in before the situation got completely out of hand, I said, "No offense intended, Mr. Mayor. We're just trying to get to see Glinda, the Good Witch of the South, and we were told that the quickest way to do so was through your beautiful town."

"Well, true, true . . ." said Mayor Rainbow. "Why did you bury the lede? If you had told me from the beginning you were friends of Glinda, we would have given you a royal welcome. She is so lovely, and we owe her so much because she protects us from marauders like you.

"OK, here's what I have to offer. All of you hop on the glass multi-colored trolley coming this way. It will take you to the southern border where there is a hidden door. Riding the trolley will keep you from breaking anything else in our precious land. The trolley conductor will open the door for you in the southern wall to let you out on the other side. I'm afraid you'll have to walk from there. We have no way of getting your motor vehicle through our land without breaking our glass roads. Anyway, the land between us and the Auntie Trolls for Liberty is a very disagreeable passage. It's full of sinkholes, bogs, and marshes and covered with tall rank grass—hiking through it will be your only option."

"Thank you, thank you Mr. Mayor," I said. "Once again, please forgive us."

"Oh, no harm, no foul," said Mayor Rainbow. "Just don't come back! As the song says, 'I got along without you before I met you—gonna get along without you now!' Cheerio!"

CHAPTER XIX

Pastor Leo Finds His Peeps

P*lop! Suck! Swat! Squish! Smack! Curse! Look out! Rinse! Repeat!*
Those actions and sounds were the only communication between us for the next two hours as we forged our way through the most arduous terrain that we had encountered on our adventures through Oz. The mayor of the Frozen Chosen had not exaggerated when he told us the land beyond his was insufferable to get through.

All of us were covered in mosquito bites on any exposed flesh, and chiggers had set up apartment complexes on our ankles. I may have been wearing magic shoes and had a protective mark on my forehead, but the bugs from Hell hadn't gotten the memo to leave me alone. The only one that seemed immune to the torture was Toe-Toe since one of us had to carry her at all times because the mud in the marshes would have swallowed her whole. The train conductor had warned us to keep a sharp eye out for alligators, and if I loved Toe-Toe, I better not let her run loose until I got to higher ground.

The only things that kept us trudging on was the promise from Maria that she had various ointments in her backpack to relieve our incessant itching once we could safely find a dry patch of land, as well as the parting conversation I had with the trolley conductor when I asked him if we'd encounter any snakes.

"Does a bear piss in the woods?" he asked while having a good belly laugh at our expense. "Let's see, well, you got your diamondback water snake, your Texas coral snake, your generic rattlesnake, and not to mention that good ol' standby, the copperhead. Good luck, y'all!"

"Is it too late to convert and join the Frozen Chosen?" I asked Pastor Leo as I sadly plopped down on a knoll overlooking bald cypress trees in the swamp below us while furiously scratching my ankles to death. I didn't know which was worse—the melancholia that seemed to envelop me in its sadness or the fear of the future and not knowing what was up ahead.

"Yes!" said Pastor Leo. "You'd shrivel up and die there—trust me. First of all, they don't know the first thing about jazz. They only know German hymns from the 1800s sung without accompaniment. If they even knew the word jazz, it would be associated with sin and thus verboten. Second of all, they don't have the color brown in their paint palette."

"Yep," I said. "I definitely noticed that you and I, by our very existence, introduced the color brown to them. That explains why they were staring at us so intensely."

"Well, it is what it is," said Pastor Leo with a touch of sadness. "Anyway, it is always darkest before dawn. Hang in there, we've almost reached our destination. Dottie, you've come so far, and suffered so much—you just can't give up now. I won't abandon you and Toe-Toe and neither will the rest of your friends."

"Leo," I said as I hugged his arm, "has anyone ever told you that you'd make a wonderful pastor?"

"*Shhhh.*" said Dr. Chen. "Do you hear voices?"

"Yes," answered Maria. "They are coming from over there beyond that incline."

Pastor Leo and Dr. Chen motioned Maria and myself to stay behind while they went to check out what was happening, but we refused. If we were going to die at this stage of the journey, at least let it be together. As we drew closer, we came upon an opening containing about forty people sitting in circles discussing what appeared to be their next strategy. The first thing I noticed about them is that they were not senior citizens—they were mostly young people in their twenties and early thirties. I was just about to ask Pastor Leo if he could ascertain if they were friend or foe, when Toe-Toe growled and barked at a kitten she saw resting in a young woman's lap.

"Show yourself," demanded one of the people in the group. "What do you want?"

We all stood up with our hands in the air as Pastor Leo explained that we were indeed friends.

"Pastor Leo!" exclaimed an excited young man standing not too far from us. "It's Pastor Leo, everyone. You remember the man I told you about that I felt was the only authentic believer in Ma'on that I'd met in Oz. Us kids used to call him the No Bullshit Pastor."

Sebastian was the young man's name and he indeed was in his late twenties and had grown up in Pastor Leo's church. The last time Pastor Leo had seen Sebastian was when he went off to college in Emerald City. He never came back home.

"Sebastian," said Pastor Leo, as he grabbed the young man in a bear hug. "It's so good to see you, my man. How have you been? How are your parents?"

"My parents and I have not spoken in years," replied Sebastian. "I don't even know where they are. They became GMOMA fanatics and rejected anything and anyone who questioned their loyalty to Purple or their outlandish conspiracy theories. When I graduated, I hooked up with the resistance movement to bring down Purple, and this is where I've been ever since. Let me introduce you to everyone."

We joined the group of young people as they served us sandwiches and fruit, and listened to their stories of how they all came together as part of a generation who refused to stand by while their parents served up their community on a platter to the Purple Satan.

Most of them had grown up in Oz churches but had become atheists, agnostics, or nones (nothing in particular). They had fled their churches and disenfranchised themselves from their families because of the cruelty and the racism they saw their parents committing in the name of the Purple Witch of the West. Although there were scores of groups like theirs, this particular group was hiding out in the swamp because of a bounty that had been put on their heads by Purple.

"Is it true that Purple has been defanged?" asked Sebastian.

"You could say that," said Pastor Leo, as we all laughed. "Her piece-of-work, The Right Reverend Emerald, the Divine, has also vanished."

"Seriously," said Sebastian. "I can't tell you how much I despise that man. I worshiped at the Emerald City Cathedral when I attended college. Even fell in love with a wonderful girl who went to that church as well, but when we got serious, and I asked her to marry me, the Wizard interfered and said that Ma'on had told him that Tiffany was not destined for marriage because she was to be married to the church—a type of nun for Ma'on. She believed that asshole, and so did her parents. I left after that and never entered another church again, and I never will."

The looks on our faces as our eyes said: *"Could this be the same Tiffany? What are the chances?"*

"I think he wanted her for himself," said Sebastian bitterly. "I often found him staring at Tiffany, and the look in his eyes made my flesh crawl."

"Sebastian," said Pastor Leo, "a lot has changed at the Emerald City Cathedral. It's a new day. The church has been humbled and will have to find its way back to truth with a capital T, if it plans on surviving and being an expression of a loving and inclusive God. We were there and witnessed its destruction with our own eyes. You might want to circle back and reach out to your Tiffany. I have a hunch she and her parents will welcome you with open arms."

"Really?" asked a very excited Sebastian. "Did you meet Tiffany when you were there? Do you know if she's with someone else? I really loved that girl—I guess I never stopped."

We didn't answer any of Sebastian's questions. I changed the subject by yelling a random memory that popped into my head at that very moment: "IS THAT A COPPERHEAD?! Do you smell cucumbers? I've been told that copperheads and rattlesnakes both give off a cucumber smell."

My hysteria over an imagined venomous snake in our immediate vicinity put a pin in us revealing anything about Tiffany. Her story was not ours to tell. She would tell Sebastian what she wanted to tell him in her own time and in her own way. But we all had a very, very good feeling that he would be a major part of her healing.

The talk of better days to come now that Purple's tentacles had been cut off the minds and out of the hearts of the followers of Ma'on, and that the Wizard's perverted control of the Emerald Cathedral had been eliminated, kept us chatting for hours. All of us recognized that the people of Oz had dodged a bullet of almost losing their democracy because they had consumed so many lies and had ignored so many basic truths. We camped the night with the young people, and I went to sleep and left Pastor Leo talking with them until the wee hours of the morning.

Upon daybreak, the group of Gen Z's and Millennials departed, determined to go back to Emerald City and make a positive difference. We hugged and kissed them goodbye and promised to stay in touch, as we made our way toward the kingdom of the Good Witch of the South.

"My friends, I want to confess something," said Pastor Leo to us after we'd been hiking for some time. "I'm not going back to assume the leadership of the Emerald Cathedral. I know that's what Otto would like me to do, but I now see that is not my calling. Our generation of believers had its chance, but many of us who claimed to love God fucked it up by hitching our wagon to an evil entity who promised us everything we ever wanted if we gave her our souls. The Church of Ma'on has been given another chance. My calling in that new church are those kids, and Tiffany, and the many others like them, because at the end of the day you and I will all soon be gone, but they—*they are the ones we've been waiting for.*"

CHAPTER XX

The Auntie Trolls for Liberty

After leaving the potential leaders of Oz's future, the four of us passed through the forest that was adjacent to the swamp as Maria grilled us about riddles.

"Come on people," said Maria, when we complained we weren't retaining any of the answers to the riddles. "You're not that old. Focus! I've divided this riddle book into quarters. If we each memorize a fourth of the book, we should be able to cover anything the trolls throw at us. Dottie's future depends on this. Now, try again . . ..

"Here's an easy one: '*What can run but never walks, has a mouth but never talks, has a head but never weeps, has a bed but never sleeps?*'"

"Uh, uh, . . . my brain is fried, remember?" I said, finding this the perfect time to play the amnesia card.

"*A river!*" said Maria. "I learned this riddle in the third grade. Dottie, you get a pass on this because your memory is still patchy, but the rest of you have no excuse, especially you, Stannum—the smartest among us.

"Here's another really easy one, especially if you've ever read the classics," said Maria. '*What goes on four legs in the morning, two in the afternoon, and three in the evening?*'"

"I definitely know this one, given my stage in life," said Stannum, after a mini lag. "*It's man!* Oedipus solved the riddle of the Sphinx when he answered by saying, *'The answer is Man. As an infant, he crawls on all fours; as an adult, he walks on two legs, and in old age, he uses a walking stick.'* If I remember the legend correctly, Oedipus meets the Sphinx at the crossroads of his journey, but she won't let him pass until he solves the 'man riddle.' Everyone before Oedipus has failed to solve it, but Oedipus gets it right, which causes the Sphinx to kill herself, by throwing herself into the sea."

"Yes, yes, yes," said Maria. "I knew you could do it! Here's another one everybody: *'A cowboy rode into town on Friday. He stayed in town for three days and rode out on Friday. How was that possible?'*"

"Now you're insulting our intelligence Maria," said Pastor Leo as he kept plowing along. "It's obvious—the *horse's name was Friday.*"

I quickly got agitated by the riddle game, and said, "Well, maybe if these monsters give us several tries to guess at least one, we might make it through. But what are the chances of them giving us those odds? I sure wish there was another way."

"Remember what I told you," said Pastor Leo. "Keep the faith. Ma'on will find a way to help us—just you wait and see."

"Maria," said Pastor Leo, "there has to be something more than riddles to defeat these suckers. Why are they called trolls—aren't they human?"

"They used to be human, but they are no longer," said Maria. "They lost their humanity ages ago. They are a group of busybody aunties that was started by the Wicked Witch of the East. She's the witch who tried to kill Dottie and whose magic shoes Dottie is wearing. They were sponsored by the Wizard to keep out anyone he deemed *others*, so as to keep Oz a homogenized society—fifty-five-plus-year-old White straight people. One of the ways the Auntie Trolls for Liberty tried to accomplish their goals was by dumbing down the intelligence of Oz citizens by eliminating books that would contradict their lies. At one point, there were so many book burnings, the sky was overcast for weeks from all of the fires.

"Like the trolls in the fairy tales, the Auntie Troll members have almost turned into stone. I've heard they now live under bridges, because like the trolls of old, they fear lightning. That's because lightning exposes their cracks and has the potential to cause them to implode if they get struck by it."

"I feel like I'm studying for my medical exams all over again," said Dr. Chen. "Only this time with riddles. This is absurd!"

"Listen, people," said an irritated Maria, "if you've got a better idea for how to get past this next obstacle then I'm all ears. These Aunties for Liberty are idiots. Talk about having shit for brains—they cut off their noses to spite their faces. Valuable information was lost in their burnings, as well as their locking down of the Internet. They now don't have access to whole troves of information that they might need to survive, and this riddle book is one of them. Trust me. When it comes time, we'll kick their asses."

"And when it comes time," said Pastor Leo, "Ma'on will show up to help us. He will not abandon us."

We hunkered down and memorized sections of the **Great Riddle Book of Oz**. In fact, we were so completely lost in our concentrated efforts that we almost missed the bridge that led to the Good Witch of the South's property.

"HALT!" said one of three trolls guarding the bridge. "Who goes there?"

"Just some visitors to the land of the Good Witch of the South," replied Pastor Leo. "Are you her guards?"

"Ha!" said the lead troll. "We hate her! But she's got too much magic for us to defeat her, so we do our best to thwart her."

"Yeah, how's that been working out for us," mumbled the second troll to the first.

"Shut up, Gertrude," hissed the leader. "Remember what I told you this morning—if you're not with us, you're against us—period!"

"We hear that you have a riddle toll," said Pastor Leo, "and we are prepared to pay it by trying to guess one out of any three riddles you choose. We understand that if we guess just one correctly, you must let us pass."

The trolls sized us up, and then began to argue amongst themselves. Finally, the leader turned back to us and said, "We sense that you've laid a trap for us, so we will double back with a trap for you. We will not give you three chances—there will only be one chance. If you blow it—which we're sure you will—we will kill you. Should you guess it by some teeny, tiny chance, then you may cross the bridge. What do you say?"

"How can we trust that you won't cheat and give us the wrong answer?" I asked. "We want to win fair and square."

"I've got an idea," said Maria. "Scratch the answer of the riddle you choose onto one of those large stones, and then turn it face down so that we can't see it. Once we answer your riddle, the stone must be rolled over for all to see. Deal?"

The head troll begrudgingly agreed. After much hushed discussion, Gertrude, the disgruntled troll, scratched something into the large stone next to the bridge and rolled it between her and Pastor Leo, being careful to keep the inscription hidden.

As we faced off with each other, the head troll began to speak as she pointed to the bits and pieces of the torn-up riddle book in our hands. "We noticed that you're all carrying contraband in your hands. Well, well, well . . .. So, we've decided that the one riddle will be the Einstein Riddle, better known as 'Who Owns the Fish' riddle. It's not in your banned book, suckers. You're so screwed! Five minutes. No! Not five . . . *two minutes!* Are you ready? Spill it out, Gertrude—and only read it once!"

Gertrude opened a scroll and read the following riddle while Dr. Chen hastily transcribed it on the back of one of the pages of our study guide:

"The Brit lives in the red house. The Swede keeps dogs as pets. The Dane drinks tea.
The green house is on the left of the white house. The green house's owner drinks coffee.

*The person who smokes Pall Mall rears birds. The owner of the yellow
house smokes Dunhill. The man living in the center house drinks milk.
The Norwegian lives in the first house.
The man who smokes Blends lives next to the one who keeps cats.
The man who keeps horses lives next to the man who smokes Dunhill.
The owner who smokes Blue Master drinks beer.
The German smokes Prince.
The Norwegian lives next to the blue house.
The man who smokes Blends has a neighbor who drinks water.
Who owns the fish?"*

My heart sank inside my stomach as I listened to the most ridiculous
riddle one could imagine. As we huddled together, Dr. Chen said immediately, "First of all, *this is not a riddle*, it's a logic problem, and it is
arguably attributed to Einstein (it could have been Sir Isaac Newton), so
our riddle book won't do us any good. I vaguely remember something
similar to it from the hazing days of medical school when the upper-
classmen tried to torment the underclassmen about our intelligence. I'm
surprised these Neanderthals even know it. But for the life of me, I can
no longer remember the answer—my brain is not what it used to be.
Here's what I wrote down by putting the three main items in a quick
graph of five by five by five: There are five color of houses (red, green,
white, yellow, blue), five drinks (tea, coffee, milk, beer, water), and five
owners (British, Swedish, Danish, Norwegian, German). It is a process
of elimination. What do you think, Maria? Do you see a pattern?"

"We're waiting!" taunted the lead troll.

As I tried to concentrate with all my might—after all, it was my
quest that still needed to be discovered—I heard the lead troll whistle
the theme from the game show *Jeopardy* and I almost lost it! What a
random memory to march back into my brain at that moment—a game
show that Jonathan and I loved and used to incessantly watch together!

*"Doo, doo doo doo, doo doo doo . . . Doo doo doo doo, doo! Doo-doo-doo-
doo-doo,"* whistled the troll. "10, 9, 8, 7, 6, 5, 4, 3, 2, 1. Which one of you
has the answer? Speak now or prepare yourselves to die!"

"I do," said an excited Maria as she showed us the answer she had written down. "But first let Pastor Leo and Dr. Chen get in a good position to turn over the rock so that we all see the answer at the same time. I don't trust you Auntie Trolls as far as I can throw you."

"Sure," answered the lead troll, "as if that will do you any good."

Once the guys were in position around the stone, Maria stepped forth and put her awesome brain on display, "Drum roll, please! The answer to the riddle as to who owns the fish: *the German owns the fish by process of elimination!*"

When the stone was rolled over, there was the answer as large as day: GERMAN!

Without wasting a minute, we charged past the trolls while they screamed in anger at each other. And because trolls are notoriously untrustworthy, they decided to kill us anyway and charged after us. Suddenly, the heavens opened up, and it started to storm, raining down like a hurricane with powerful thunder and frightening lightning strikes. When we heard blood-curdling screams, we looked back and saw each of the trolls struck by bolts of lightning. It was just as Pastor Leo said he would: Ma'on had showed up.

CHAPTER XXI

Dottie Meets Glinda the Good Witch

By the time we got to the end of the bridge, we were soaking wet but out of the storm. When we looked back, the storm was still raging around the trolls as they exploded into a gazillion pieces of stone.

We hobbled away from the carnage as fast as we could, which really wasn't very fast at this point. Dr. Chen had lost his cane on the bridge and painfully twisted his ankle. My ankles and feet were so swollen from the chigger bites and those damn magic shoes that I could barely scoot, let alone walk. Somewhere between the Emerald City and the Gnarly Forrest, I'd lost my blood pressure meds, and I could tell the stress had elevated my pressure to the moon because I had heart palpitations. Pastor Leo's bursitis had flared up in the hip that hadn't been replaced yet. The only two who didn't look too worse for wear were Maria and Toe-Toe, who Maria now had to carry because my hands were too swollen with fluid retention from eating too much salty beef jerky and not drinking enough water. I was beginning to think that we were the butt of some cosmic joke because who in their right mind would create an adventure featuring a septuagenarian, a sexagenarian, and an octogenarian, and the only ones left who could still function properly were the quinquagenarian and a one-year-old puppy.

Slowly, slowly, we made our way to the edge of the forest. Finally, as we parted the branches of the most magnificent willow trees I'd ever seen, we saw a lovely cottage in the distance surrounded by an immaculate garden of roses, gardenia bushes, and azaleas. We staggered up to the inviting door and I knocked on it. My knock was answered by a very warm and welcoming indigenous grandmother-type who looked at us with a smile and eyes that seemed to say: "Welcome, what took you so long?"

"Please excuse our intrusion," I said wearily. "We are here for an audience with Glinda, the Good Witch of the South. Could you point us in the direction that we should go?"

"No, darlin'," said the cheerful native woman, holding open the door and beckoning us to come through. "Not before I feed you. You are clearly strangers who have come from a long way off and you look like you're starving. Your Chinese friend looks as if his ankle is in so much pain he can barely stand. Sit down and take a load off. Her Highness will wait for you."

Dr. Chen whispered to us that he recognized our hostess as a descendent of the Tāp Pīlam Coahuiltecan Nation. He was over the moon to meet her and discover new information about her culture. Our hostess introduced herself as Atina, which meant "mother." She then proceeded to serve us a fabulous stew with freshly baked bread, three kinds of cakes, two plates of cookies, and a bowl of mashed cornbread, vegetables, and diced chicken for Toe-Toe.

"How far is it to the Good Witch of the South's castle, Atina?" I asked.

"Not too far," said Atina. "And around here, we have dropped her formal title because she is so benevolent. We call her Glinda the Good. Just take that road to the right of my cottage, walk to the south, and you will soon come upon her castle."

When we had been fully refreshed, we thanked our gracious hostess and headed south. As we passed several lovely fields and crossed over two beautiful wooden bridges, a transformation began to happen with us. We all noticed that the closer we got to Glinda's castle, the less we suffered from our previously noted maladies. By the time we approached the gate of a very beautiful castle, miraculously Dr. Chen no longer limped, Pastor Leo's hip was no longer acting up, and my hands, ankles, and feet no longer looked like I was starring in *The Elephant Man*. Even our clothes were magically cleaned and pressed, and we were so stunned that, when the head sergeant of the all-female patrol that guarded Glinda the Good's castle approached us, we could hardly speak.

"Why have you come to the South Country?" asked the head sergeant.

"To see Glinda the Good, who rules here," I sputtered.

"Let me have your names and I will see if she will meet with you," said the sergeant.

The sergeant returned within minutes and told us that Glinda the Good had said that she'd been expecting us and that we should be admitted immediately.

We were escorted into Glinda the Good's throne room. It was hard not to gawk at the beauty of the royal hall. The walls were covered in a periwinkle fabric with a rich gold trim. From the ceiling hung four massive chandeliers, and on either side of the Persian-carpeted runway were eight navy blue, velvet-stuffed, and tasseled ottomans trimmed in gold ribbon. The throne was at the end of the room perched upon a platform that was four steps up. Glinda's throne chair was covered by a canopy of embroidered blue jays and yellow finches and the tassels attached to the canopy were made of blue and yellow embroidery threads.

Glinda the Good was the most beautiful woman any of us had ever seen. When we discussed meeting her afterwards, we all agreed she was of mixed race, but none of us could determine what races. To Dr. Chen, she looked part Chinese and part African. To me, she looked part African and part Caucasian. To Maria, Glinda looked part Latina and part African. To Pastor Leo, she looked part African and part Scandinavian.

None of us could determine her age—she simply looked timeless.

Her hair was jet black with sprinkles of diamonds all through it, and it hung in soft ringlets around her face and in loose coils down to her waist. We could never determine the exact color of her eyes, as they changed from ice blue, to green, to hazel, to brown, and to stormy black. When she stood to come down off her throne to meet us as we bowed before her, we all swore she was seven feet tall.

When she stood in front of me, she lifted my chin so that I could look into her eyes, and said, "Welcome, Dorothy Hope Gale. It is such a delight to meet you."

I smiled back at her, but I was unable to say a word.

"It is such an honor to finally meet you all," Glinda said, as Pastor Leo, Dr. Chen, and Maria introduced themselves. "Ma'on has told me so much about you, and how proud he is of how you all worked so tirelessly and courageously and saved Oz from the lies and cruelty that had enslaved it. Bravo to you all!

"Dottie, I understand from my mother, who fed you lunch, that you have a request for me," said Glinda.

"Yes, your Highness, I do," I replied. "Toe-Toe and I just want to find where we belong. Since Jonathan's murder, we have been aimless. I have come to believe that people perish when they have no home and no sense of belonging. Would you please help us?"

"My dear, you and Toe-Toe have always had the power to find out where you belong," said Glinda. "The power was in the silver shoes. All you have to do is click your heels three times together, and your memory will be fully restored, and the place where you belong will be revealed."

Now that the time had actually come for my dream to be fulfilled, I was overwhelmingly frightened. What if I didn't like the remaining memories that would return? What if tomere I belonged wasn't where I wanted to be?

I turned to my friends—my boon companions—and we all burst into tears as we clung to each other for dear life in what seemed like forever.

"It's time. Turn around and face me, Dottie," said Glinda the

Good. "Now, close your eyes, hold onto Toe-Toe real tight, and listen to my voice very carefully.

"Click your heels three times and say, *'Take me to where I truly belong. Reveal to me my home!'*"

Just as I was instructed—with my eyes closed, and facing Glinda the Good—I clicked my heels three times and said: "Take me to where I truly belong. Reveal to me my home!"

Out of the mouth of Glinda, came the words I'd heard so often through the years: *"Don't give up, Miss Fine Thang. Stay loving, stay caring, stay humble, and the good things of life will lift you into the place where you belong."*

Without missing a beat and not even thinking about what I was saying, I smiled and replied, *"Yeah, right back at you, girlfriend!"*

My eyes popped open at the recognition of *that voice*. The silver magic clogs flew off my feet. Toe-Toe started barking as if her very life depended on me understanding what she was trying to say. Then for a split second, Glinda's face morphed into Jonathan's, and then switched back into her own.

I hugged and kissed Toe-Toe with all my might, as I whispered softly into her ear, "Did you see her Toe-Toe, baby? Did you see your mommy's face?"

A rush of warm air wrapped itself around my body, and I had this overwhelming sense of well-being—a sense that where Toe-Toe and I were now was exactly where we belonged, and our quest had brought us to a very happy ending, indeed.

The End . . . (um, not quite!)

EPILOGUE

From the Diary of Glinda,
The Good Witch

Today, my kingdom is celebrating the lives of four—no, five—extraordinary beings who became heroes in Oz, and who I had the pleasure to meet a century ago. Statues now dot the land from top to bottom in honor of them. But the statues don't tell the entire story—the happily-ever-after ending of their collective narrative. As one of the immortals who has lived among the mortals of Oz since the beginning, I cheered these precious humans on to their final God-given destinies. I wondered if this time in human history, this group of frail beings would be able to sound the clarion call loud enough to awaken their families, friends, and neighbors—who had fallen under the spell of a narcissistic wicked witch—to the imminent demise of their democracy if they didn't wake up in time.

◆

The Land of Oz almost came undone. What started as a land full of hope and promise for all, that boasted of being a shining city on a hill, increasingly became a city whose lights began to dim and burn out. Its religious people turned their backs on their better angels, and Oz would have been destroyed had it not been for a handful of the most unlikely heroes.

Where are those heroes now?

Dr. Stannum 'Tin' Chen and Maria went back to Emerald City and converted the Emerald Cathedral into a first-class mental health facility for those who had been traumatized by abuse of all kinds—especially sexual abuse. They married within a year of retrofitting the cathedral, and I was the officiate at their wedding. It was beautiful to see the heart of Dr. Chen expand to include so much more love in his life as his precious Daiyu had encouraged him to do. Dr. Chen lived to be ninety-nine years old and worked until the day he died—all of his mental faculties perfectly intact. The only physical malady that returned was his limp, after all, mortal bodies do eventually wear out. But Maria helped him assuage what Dr. Chen called, "a slight annoyance," by keeping his closet stocked with a bevy of uniquely carved canes.

Maria Espantapájaro went back to school and eventually became the medical doctor she always dreamed about becoming. After Dr. Chen died, Maria continued to carry on his work, and she never, ever doubted that she had a very excellent brain again.

Sebastian and Tiffany reconnected, rekindled the love that was never lost—just bruised—and under the healing guidance of Dr. Chen and Maria, married a few years later. Pastor Leo was the officiate at their wedding, and it was quite the emotional affair. Tiffany decorated the entire green cathedral—ceiling to floor—in pink, which gave us all such joy. Maria was the matron of honor, Dottie and her jazz band performed during the ceremony and the reception, and Toe-Toe was the ring bearer. Otto gave his daughter away, but he blubbered so uncontrollably as he walked down the aisle, that Astrid and all their kids had to join him midway to keep that dear man from collapsing as the horror of what might have been washed over his psyche. Sebastian and Tiffany eventually had two kids—a boy and a girl. Sebastian also ran for president of Oz, which he won, hands down, and served two terms. He was a good and

*honorable ruler and set the standard for the type of leader Oz should culti-
vate in the future. Sebastian and Tiffany mentored many young people to
rise up into leadership in Oz's government as their parents' generation
died off.*

*__Pastor Leo__ became an itinerant preacher and pastor and never
settled down in one place. He said his church was wherever the bruised and
hurting next generation needed him. However, because of Pastor Leo's
humble example of godly leadership where cruelty and meanness had once
been the order of the day as espoused by the so-called followers of Ma'on, he
became the standard bearer of Ma'on's love, truth, humility, compas-
sionate inclusivity, mercy, and justice. Over time, other wonderful Ma'on
leaders soon followed in Leo's footsteps. From time to time, when Pastor
Leo needed a sabbatical, he would return to my kingdom. Those were some
of my sweetest times—when Leo, Dottie, and I spent laughter-filled
evenings watching the sun go down while sampling the latest wines
produced from my vineyard.*

*__Jonathan "Glinda" Dubois,__ as I was assured by Ma'on, was
finally able to rest in peace on Earth and get on with his eternal calling as
an entertainer in the great beyond, once he knew his sweet Dottie and baby
Toe-Toe were well taken care of. Jonathan got the ball rolling. Had it not
been for Jonathan's initial courage to stand up and fight against the evil
consuming the land that he loved, all might have been lost. He was a drag
queen extraordinaire—a top-notch entertainer before he died. But more
than that, he was a good and decent human being who gave his life so the
people of Oz would fulfill their land's purpose. What's more, I'm told she
does a killer performance imitating me on a regular basis in the eternal
realm. I've been meaning to stop by and check out her act, but I'm in no
rush because I do have all of eternity.*

*__Dorothy Hope Gale__ came to live with me in my kingdom. I had a
beautiful cottage built for her with a glorious flower garden that she
helped plan and plant. Dottie built a lucrative jazz career performing
throughout Oz at sold-out concerts until her health began to fail. She never
traveled beyond the borders of Oz to perform because she said she couldn't
bear being apart from her baby. Toe-Toe died at least a decade before*

Dottie stopped performing, and we buried her precious companion at the foot of a weeping willow tree that grew by the stream that meanders behind Dottie's cottage. A week before Dottie died, Maria came to visit Dottie in her home. As I entered the back door of the house to say hello, I overheard Maria ask Dottie if she was afraid of dying, and she responded, "No, not at all, my love."

"So, what do you think happens to us when we die?" asked Maria.

"We go home, darling . . . we go home!"

DEFINITELY *THE END* THIS TIME

ᴀCKNOWLEDGMENTS

I owe a huge debt of gratitude to L. Frank Baum whose magical tale, **The Wonderful Wizard of Oz** inspired this book. Although I twisted Baum's wizard inside out in my reimagining of his fairy tale, I think the author would have approved if he were living today through these trying times with our country on the verge of losing its democracy, if his story could be used to remove the scales from the eyes of the blind and unplug the ears of the deaf before it is too late.

A special thanks to my very incredible supportive readers and for those who helped make this book possible. This includes Karen S., Larry C., Dottie L. (thanks for the loan of your name D), Paul T., and Maxine W. A special shout out to Steve Bennett from AuthorBytes who introduced me to Charles Levin of Munn Avenue Press, as well as a shout out to Charlie's team, all of whom worked tirelessly and efficiently to creatively flesh out my vision of reimagining a classic tale as a warning trumpet for our troubled times.

I tip my hat to my baby sister, Cynthia R., who in her golden years serves the underserved, and daily reminds me by her actions that there is no unworthy person—no *us* and *them*—we are all God's children worthy of love, and we're never too old to bring grace to the Earth. She was my first cheerleader from the age of four, and I'm convinced that I'm still standing because of her continued, unwavering support and belief in my talents, and in me as a human being.

Most importantly, I have to thank my incredible kids, K & C, who steadfastly held up my arms in support of my burning desire to try and make a difference during these awful, gaslighted times in the hopes that

I could join the collective group of truth-tellers who are trying to leave a better world for the next generation. They've taught me so much about unconditional love and helped me expand my tent pegs of love. It's because of them that I might actually end this journey well—that I might become the person God created me to be. *("My Little Women, I love you both—madly!")*

I dedicate this book to my precious grandchildren (F and C) as a beacon of hope and encouragement that they might do a better job than my generation did in representing the true heart of God on Earth.

Last, but never least, I want to thank my wonderful husband, JT, whom I've known for fifty-one-plus years, and whom I've been married to for forty-five-plus years. I married a White man; he married a Black woman, and I am convinced our marriage has made a beautiful difference in this oftentimes ugly, hateful world. We both loved each other unconditionally through our wounds to wholeness. He has never failed to tirelessly support me in all my endeavors. To him I say: *"Je t'aimerai pour toujours parce que tu es mon cœur et ma maison."*

About the Author

Eleanor Tomczyk is a memoirist and humorist blogger whose work features the musings of an engagingly funny ex-Evangelical Conservative Christian, African-American Baby Boomer. At the age of 60, the wife, mother, grandmother, singer, actress, motivational speaker, and award-winning voice-over artist set out to establish a new career in retirement as a storyteller, using her life and her journey through White Conservative churches as fodder. Currently in her mid-70s, the mother, grandmother, and wife of 45+ years has published four books: **Monsters' Throwdown** (2013), **Fleeing Oz** (2015), **The Fetus Chronicles: Podcasts to My Fetus-self** (2017), and **House of Oz Undone: A Cautionary Tale** (2024). She also posts a humorous, political weekly blog: *How the Hell Did I End Up Here?* In 2022, the author wrote the following prayer and posted it on her vision board:

"Dear Lord: I want to write a book that is so widely read and seen that it helps break the Taliban-like stronghold on many White Evangelical Conservative Christian churches which are currently committing adultery with fascism and authoritarianism—an **Uncle Tom's Cabin,** *so to speak —to start a figurative civil war against lies being told in the name of Jesus. I want my words to join a revolution of truth and love in the readers' hearts that set all people free to live transformative lives of true love, freedom, mercy, grace, and truth instead of the hypocrisy currently masquerading as Christianity in many parts of the Body of Christ and defaming the true loving nature of Jesus.*

"P.S. Please hurry God! I'm already 73—not much time left for the task at hand."

www.ingramcontent.com/pod-product-compliance
Lightning Source LLC
Chambersburg PA
CBHW030147010826
48973CB00002B/768